ABOUT THIS BOOK

With his hard rock band Pink Melon nominated for a Grammy, lead singer Brett Rhys-Falwyck's dreams are about to come true. Then tragedy strikes. After losing the one person he loves most, he turns to the only thing he knows will never fail him—his music. But even that's betrayed by the corrupt owner of the band's management company that owns his soul. Turning his back on his bandmates, he finds himself in the mountains of Colorado— running a band camp, of all things.

Cecelia Amundson, angel and owner of Havenwood Falls Music & More, can't stop dreaming of a man she's never met. Knowing he needs her help, she invites him to Havenwood Falls to run a music camp sponsored by her store. As soon as he arrives, she senses a darkness gripping his soul and curling its hooks deeper inside him.

In a race to save his soul, Cecelia grows ever closer to Brett. But she must hold tight to her heart, for within this tortured man lies a secret darker than her past, and deadlier than she ever imagined.

HAVENWOOD FALLS BOOKS

Forget You Not by Kristie Cook

Old Wounds by Susan Burdorf

Fate, Love & Loyalty by E.J. Fechenda

The Winged & the Wicked by T.V. Hahn & Kristie Cook

Alpha's Queen by Lila Felix

Ink & Fire by R.K. Ryals

Lose You Not by Kristie Cook

Tragic Ink by Heather Hildenbrand

Nowhere to Hide by Belinda Boring

Flames Among the Frost by Amy Hale

Rock Me Gently by Susan Burdorf

From the Embers by Amy Miles

Defying Gravity by Kallie Ross

Break Me Not by Kristie Cook

How the Dead Lie by Stacey Rourke

The Lurkers Within by Danielle Bannister

The Collector: Awakening by Kristie Cook, R.K. Ryals, Belinda Boring & Nadirah Foxx

Addicted to You by Belinda Boring

Affliction Mine by C.J. Pinard

The Ward & the Wanderers by T.V. Hahn

Toil & Trouble by Melissa Wright

Of Salt and Stars by Seven Jane

Redefined by Morgan Wylie

Betrayal Among the Frost by Amy Hale

Forever Loyal by E.J. Fechenda

Fate's Demand by Emily Cyr

The Wu & the Wand by T.V. Hahn

A Demon's Redemption by JD Nelson

Also try the YA line, Havenwood Falls High; the historical paranormal line, Legends of Havenwood Falls; the darker, sexier side of town, Havenwood Falls Sin & Silk; and the local supernatural college, Sun & Moon Academy.

Stay up to date at www.HavenwoodFalls.com

ROCK ME GENTLY

A HAVENWOOD FALLS NOVEL

SUSAN BURDORF

To Kristie Cook and all the folks at Havenwood Falls. What a magical town!

LOVE IS LIKE A MEMORY

(PINK MELON: ONE TIME MORE)

Written and sung by Brett Rhys-Falwyck

What happened to our story
Your love is like a memory
I kiss you but you aren't there
I reach for you but hold only air
Mmm ooo mmm ooo
Your love is like a memory
Mmm ooo mmm ooo
Your love is like a memory
What happened to the kisses we shared
Our lips meeting, the souls we bared
I touched your heart, and you touched mine
We promised our love would last for all time
Mmm ooo mmm ooo
Your love is like a memory
Mmm ooo mmm ooo
Your love is like a memory
Our love is like a ghost

That haunts me more than most
I fly to you, but you touch the sun
And go, and go, a fire never won
Mmm ooo mmm ooo
Your love is like a memory
Mmm ooo mmm ooo
Your love is like a memory
Are you an illusion? A myth?
What do you hold a firefly with
I want to keep you in a jar
I want to know who we are
Mmm ooo mmm ooo
Your love is like a memory
Mmm ooo mmm ooo
Your love is like a memory
So please, oh please come back to me
I will take you as you are, not a memory
For our love will survive all time
I am yours and you are mine
Mmm ooo mmm ooo
Your love is like a memory
Mmm ooo mmm ooo
Your love is like a memory

CHAPTER 1

"*H*ey, Brett, you ready?"

Brett Rhys-Falwyck, lead guitarist and singer for the band Pink Melon, looked left, then nodded. Looking to his right, he nodded again. Slipping the ear buds into his ears so he could keep in touch with their sound crew, he stepped forward and pulled the microphone closer. Striking the opening chord of their multi-platinum hit song "Love Is Like a Memory," he lowered his tone and sang to the enthusiastic screams and cheers from the thousands of fans in the arena as they recognized and approved his song choice.

Lights flashed around them, psychedelic and random, adding a heartbeat to the drumbeat and chords ramping up the audience's enthusiasm. Not that they needed much more to get them dancing. From the minute Brett and the boys of Pink Melon stepped onto the stage and began the opening to their hit that was flooding the airwaves, the audience belonged to them.

Brett's body gyrated provocatively, caught up in the deep bass and fast rhythms of the song and sending the audience into a frenzy of movement that matched his subtle sexuality. He didn't notice.

Throwing his head back and hips forward, he strummed his guitar with a fierce desire to wring every note from the instrument, as if stroking a lover's body. Smooth and sure, his fingers slid and caressed each string, pulling from the guitar the emotion of the song as if he were playing for every woman in the audience individually.

He ignored the whistles and screams from the bobbing crowd below the stage, focusing instead on the song's words and their meaning, trying to draw every bit of feeling out of the song that he could. Nothing stopped him when he became like this. He smiled as the spotlights flashed on and off the other band members, keeping them in both shadow and light, further adding to the unreality of being in a full house with adoring fans screaming their names. He saw his bandmates, all of them friends for quite a while before the band hit it big, enjoying the music and adulation from the crowd as much as he was. Were they inspired by his energy, or by their own connection to the music? In the end, that wasn't as important as giving the audience what they paid for.

The audience was hearing even more than that tonight. His body absorbed the music, the tune singing in his blood and lending a fire to his playing he hadn't heard before. He was inspired to be greater, his late mother's presence all around him, comforting and familiar, pushing him to new heights. He felt nine years old again with his first guitar playing just to her, even though the audience in front of him strained for his attention.

This particular song was one he and the band had argued about before coming on stage. He wanted to open with it, but the others wanted to end with it, to keep the audience anticipating whether they would play it or not. He'd won that particular battle as scheduling the set order was his thing, after all. He instinctively knew what the crowd would go for, and he'd yet to be proven wrong.

The song was up for a Grammy Award and very popular at

concerts even though, as a ballad, it was very different from most of what they played. Pink Melon wasn't known for playing love songs. Their fans expected more rock and roll with hard chords and riffs, but this song had somehow captured the attention of radio stations across the country, and that had led to fans requesting it on the online outlets. Their music video had over a million views, all of which helped shoot the song up the charts and skyrocket the band to prominence.

Their newest album would have more ballads and less rock and roll due to his songs. That had led to a bit of discord among the guys. Grumbling, they'd played their parts, sang his lyrics, but still they didn't like the direction the band was going. Brett was sure they would be talking about this for a while before they went on tour again, this time to bigger houses, they hoped. No more college campuses or state fairs or small venues unless they chose them.

Brett leaned into the microphone, his mouth nearly sucking it like a lollipop as he locked eyes with a pretty redhead in the crowd. She danced for him as he sang, her large boobs nearly falling out of her low-cut T-shirt as she sought to keep his attention. The light moved on, and she was lost to view in the sudden darkness.

The crowd cheered and sang along to the popular tune. The song, one Brett had penned when in one of his rare romantic moments, had become such a sensation that the band was nonstop busy these days. No one was complaining. Playing to sold-out houses had been the goal of Pink Melon from the beginning, after all. Rock and roll might be what put them together, but romantic ballads like this one were going to pay the bills. They all knew it— didn't like it, but knew it.

As the song progressed, Brett alternately singing and strumming his guitar to the subtle rhythms of the unique love song, the rest of the band played to the crowd with their own enthusiastic gyrations and musical accompaniments.

The crowd cheered enthusiastically every time Cooly dipped his guitar or flipped his long blond hair like an eighties rocker. The other band members—drummer Peter "Sticks" Friend and their keyboardist Harry Williams—also bobbed and swayed to the music.

Brett glanced out into the nearly invisible audience. The redhead, if she was still there, was hidden in the glare of the lights. He couldn't see anyone in particular right now, just indefinable shapes as the lights scanned the crowd like a police helicopter, making individual faces impossible to differentiate. Closing his eyes to lose the feeling of vertigo that always struck him when on stage, he took a deep breath and focused on his guitar and the music instead of the overexcited fans.

The combination of the footlights, hot smells from the electrical equipment, the sharp familiar feel of his guitar, and its steel strings on his fingers lulled him into a kind of melodic trance. He knew where he was, but he became lost in his music—a trait reporters following the music scene called his "harmonic haze," but which he called his "escape." Music had always been a way to express thoughts and emotions too painful or uncomfortable to talk about face to face with the people in his life.

Shy and a bit of a loner, starting a band was a way to challenge himself out of his shell. His mother had often despaired of ever receiving grandchildren from her shy only child, and her recent death from cancer made that a real regret for him. Biting his lip, he relished the pain that kept him in the moment. Fighting back the tears that threatened to fall at the thought of his mother, he closed his eyes, taking deep ragged breaths to regain control of his emotions. How she would have loved to be here, front and center, for his performance. He regretted so much in life, nothing more than the fact that she would never be here to share this with him.

His focus returned to the strings, the solidness of the guitar, and the energy he felt in the air around him as he put the sadness of his mother's death behind him. His heart pounding, his body vibrating with the release music always brought to him, his attention returned to the music.

Every time he sang this song, he felt he was sending out a message to someone, but who? Someone he'd never met? Someone he wanted to meet? He was never sure, but he knew—judging by the thousands of posts and Twitter comments from lonely women and men too—that his message of love being lost and searched for was reaching into the souls of the people he sang to.

So many lonely people.

And he was one of them.

As the final note of the last encore song echoed out, Pink Melon left the stage, another successful concert in the books. Behind the stage, they smiled, talked to fans, took innumerable photos with the lucky fans who won backstage passes from local radio stations, and did interviews for rock magazines.

"Finally," Brett sighed as he closed the door to the band's dressing room, "a few minutes of peace."

Taking advantage of the time before the rest of the band joined him, he collapsed onto the couch facedown, closing his eyes, trying as best he could to shut out the world.

Breathing deeply, he tried to find the place he always returned to in his thoughts, his serenity place, the imaginary place he went to when the world became too heavy to bear.

The mountains were so beautiful tonight. Lit by the silver glow of the moon, the scene spread before him was perfect. Cool breezes ruffled his hair, and the strong, acrid scent of pine and the subtler odor of fresh turned soil surrounded him like a familiar coat. The cares of the day slipped from his body like water after a shower. The delicate sounds of the night carried with them a subtle music of their own making that wrapped around his mind, pulling from him the troubles that rested on his shoulders like boulders. He was more at peace than at any time he had been that day.

Glancing around the forest of his imagination, he walked a short distance across grass that brushed his ankles, sending up waves of a clean and crisp fragrance he found soothing and refreshing. Ahead of him, a path unfolded from the vegetation as if inviting him to tread upon it.

Walking around the bend in the path, he found himself facing a large boulder that rested on the edge of a cliff. Something about that stone drew him closer. Peering over the side, he saw a drop-off that ended a few hundred feet below. He noticed a narrow river that reflected the moonlight like molten silver.

This is new, he thought. He watched the water flow gently on its way to who knew where. The air was so still, he could hear the rush of water that signaled a waterfall might be near, but he couldn't see it. Looking over his shoulder, he noticed the thick grass near the boulder's edge. He sat with his back against the rock and closed his eyes. Breathing deeply of the scents of this verdant area of the forest, his dream self was nearly asleep when soft footfalls interrupted his meditative state.

Opening his eyes, he was shocked to see a petite woman with a long blond ponytail standing at the edge of the precipice. She wore a body-hugging, dark-colored jogging suit, the reflective stripes catching the morning sun and shining back at him like a beacon. As he watched—afraid to move lest he startle her, even though he was still asleep and couldn't really touch her—she unzipped the jacket, revealing a tank top that molded itself to her body. Her breasts were small, and her waist, accentuated by the clinging fabric, was tiny. Dropping the jacket next to her on the grass, she flexed her powerful-looking shoulders in the low-backed tank top she wore. A strange glow appeared around her in a soft silvery hue, and her tank top seemed to flow and grow around her until she shook her head, her hair slipping from the ponytail to pour down her back like a golden river.

In profile, he barely saw her face, but what he did see caused him to gasp. She was more than beautiful. Highlighted by the light, she was almost the answer to a prayer. As she turned back around, she lifted her arms to the sky. She stretched and shook her body slightly as if to free the flesh of invisible bonds.

He gasped as her shoulder blades elongated, then unfolded into wings. Wings! Beautiful ivory-colored wings, with feathers so soft and delicate, he wanted to reach out and stroke them.

To his surprise, she turned to look at him, her face backlit by a glow that hid her features and outlined her body. He heard her voice, soft and gentle in his mind as she said, "Come to Havenwood Falls. Seek thy peace within its comforting embrace. You will find her there."

She reached out a hand to him as if inviting him to join her, but he hesitated, and the moment was lost.

"Where? Who? Who will I find there?" his dream self answered her.

But she only smiled in response. Turning, she spread her wings, waving them back and forth like a newborn butterfly trying to dry them, but they didn't appear wet at all. The breeze was a gentle caress on his tortured soul as she lifted effortlessly from the ground. He rose, arms outstretched as if to catch her, certain she would fall, but instead, she flew upward, disappearing into the sky overhead. He stood, bracing himself against the rock, searching for her, but she was gone.

Brett woke with a start, his mind still fuzzy and unclear. Where was Havenwood Falls? Who would be there waiting for him? What did this strange dream mean? He'd never dreamt of angels before. Was she his mother sending him a message? Or was she the result of too many tacos earlier?

Brett lost his grip on the dream as the voices of his bandmates entering the room brought him back to the present with a disorienting snap. He grabbed the sides of his head and rested his elbows on his knees as he regained control of his breathing.

Peter walked in, chatting excitedly to Cooly and Sticks about the concert. The three were unaware of Brett's confused state until Cooly looked over at him, a frown on his face.

"Hey, man, you were inspired tonight," Cooly said. He slapped his friend on the back and squeezed Brett's shoulder for good measure before moving over to see if any of the pre-show snacks were left. The table was pretty bare of all but some celery sticks and dip. Making a face, Cooly took a bite before setting the rest of the celery back on the table.

Brett ignored him as he sat up straighter, the last vestiges of the dream slipping away, and the words *Havenwood Falls* echoing in his mind in a weird rhythm not unlike a lullaby. He tried to find the peace he'd held onto for all of twenty minutes, but it was gone. He couldn't be mad for too long at Cooly, though. A lot of history was there between the two of them.

Cooly was, of course, his nickname. His real name was Edward Cole, and he was a classmate of Brett's from Western Kentucky University, where both he and Brett had gone to college. Eddie was to become an accountant and Brett a teacher, but once they'd formed Pink Melon, neither had had the time to continue their education.

The band had become their future. They'd added two local guys, Peter "Sticks" Friend and Harry Williams, and the quartet had played local clubs in and around WKU until they'd struck fire with Brett's original songs. The songs had earned them a record deal with a small independent studio out of Nashville, Tennessee, and the rest was history still being written.

While Harry and Sticks argued in a corner about the conquests they wanted for the evening, Cooly touched Brett on the arm to get his attention. "What's up, Brett? And don't tell me there's nothing going on. I've known you too long to believe that, man."

"Everything's fine," Brett reassured his friend. He lowered his eyes, blinking rapidly as he relived the dream. What did it mean?

"Now?" asked Peter. The three other band members were looking at each other guiltily, and Brett straightened slightly.

"Now, what?" Brett asked, an edge to his voice that surprised him. He was definitely more disturbed by the dream than he'd thought if he was talking in this tone to his friends.

None of the others appeared to want to be the first to speak. Their glances became more pointed until finally, with a deep sigh, Eddie spoke.

"Brett . . . I've been thinking . . . I mean we've been thinking . . . well, it's just . . ." Eddie couldn't get the words out.

"Spit it out, Cooly. What's going on?"

"Listen, Brett, we all appreciate the way you've taken the band to where we are, heck, we've got a Grammy Award show to appear on in just a few days, but . . . well . . . ," Peter said, faltering at the end.

"We want to take a break," Harry finished.

Brett looked between his friends, confusion on his face.

"The death of your mom hit you hard, man," Cooly said softly, touching Brett on the arm. "We all get that, but the band is going places we don't want to go. We thought maybe after the Grammys appearance, we could just take a break. It's nothing personal. We just . . ." His voice trailed off at the end as he raised his hands in defeat.

"You want to break up the band?" Brett stared at them all in disbelief.

"No, no, not at all," all three jumped in to reassure Brett.

"We just want to take a breather. Gather our thoughts and all that," Cooly said.

"Told you he'd freak," Peter muttered.

"I'm not freaking," Brett said coldly. He stood and paced in front of his friends, disbelief on his face. "But I gotta say this has hit me out of the blue. I mean, we're finally at the place we always wanted to be. We have a hit song, a couple Grammy nominations.

We're living the dream, man, and you want to call it quits? I don't get it." Brett was warming up to his anger.

Cooly grabbed Brett's arm and spun him around to face him. "We're not splitting up the band. We just need a break. We need to regroup, figure out where we want the band to go. We can't do that if we are constantly traveling. Some of us"—he pointed to Peter and Harry—"have other plans for the band. We need to find our direction."

"Bands that go on 'hiatus' don't usually come back," Brett said coldly.

"We know," muttered Peter. "But honestly, Brett, that's not what we want."

Brett glared at them all. "So, who will go solo first?" he spat out, not keeping the anger out of his tone.

"No one. I'm planning to go chase some waves," Peter said. "I haven't surfed in a couple years. I just want a life, Brett. Surely you do, too? Especially since your mother's death . . ."

Brett raised a hand. "Don't you dare drag my mother's death into this. Jesus Christ, I didn't even get to go to her funeral because we were on the road."

"We know," said Cooly with a calmness that just made Brett angrier. "But that was what got us all thinking about what we were giving up. Harry is trying to get back together with Tony, but being on the road is making that hard. I have family I haven't seen in weeks, and Skype conversations don't cut it anymore. We just want a life again. Don't you?"

Brett's shoulders slumped. One of the prices of success was that you had to dedicate yourself totally to the project you were on or it wouldn't work. Rock 'n' roll was a hard business, and would suck you dry if you let it.

Looking at his three friends, he could see their distress. They were exhausted. They wanted—no, they deserved—a break.

Slumping into a chair, he nodded.

"I get it. So we do the Grammys and then we're off for a bit?"

Everyone grinned and nodded, knowing they'd won the battle.

"So what do you think you're going to do, Brett?" Cooly asked him later as they packed up to head out.

"Maybe go skiing. There's this place I heard of, Havenwood Falls; guess I might see about going there."

"Never heard of it," Cooly said. "Where is it?"

"No clue," Brett admitted, "but maybe I can go there to forget about all this."

With that cryptic comment, he got into his car, slammed the door, and drove off without a backward glance.

An hour later when he arrived home, Brett climbed the stairs to his house and gathered up his mail.

A small glossy brochure fell to the floor at his feet. Bending down to pick it up, he stared in shock when he saw the words *Havenwood Falls* in large font across the front. Skiers, tall paper cups of coffee in their hands, invited him to enjoy the magic of Colorado. There was a phone number on the bottom of the brochure for a place to rent cabins.

"That's . . . weird," he thought as he tossed the flyer on the island and went to the fridge, where he pulled out a large beer, popped the cap, and chugged the contents. As he wiped his mouth, his eyes fell on the brochure again. Picking it up, he studied it for a minute before shaking his head.

Even though he'd told Cooly he was thinking about going there, he'd only been joking. Now though, staring at the brochure, he wasn't so sure the joke wasn't on him.

THE UNEXPECTEDNESS OF YOU

(PINK MELON: ONE TIME MORE)

Written and sung by Brett Rhys-Falwyck

Life is full of the surprises that bring light to day
We hope for secrets
but we get truth instead
I run in circles, worry about the nonsense
You bring an anchor to my journey
I let you go
I let you go
The unexpectedness of you was always the way
You could walk in a room, filling it with laughter
and leave me with nothing but tears
but I would wish for nothing less
All the agony, the pain, are worth your kisses
I let you go
I let you go
If I ever have the chance to love that way again
I hope it is with you

CHAPTER 2

*C*ecelia Eurydice Amundson set the sheet music on the counter and sighed. Yawning deeply, she closed her eyes and fought the urge to close the shop and go back to bed. Running Havenwood Falls Music & More was a labor of love most days, but lately she found herself tired and wishing for sleep, something angels rarely needed.

The dreams had been coming more and more frequently lately, and she wasn't sure what that meant. The man in her dreams was usually lost in shadow and darkness, but he didn't feel threatening, just watching and waiting. He also felt familiar, but she couldn't place who he was, or where she might have seen him before. She was certain he had not been to Havenwood Falls before, though. With his long dark hair, rock-hard body, and sensual mouth, she was sure she would remember him if she'd ever met him before.

His lean body was always poised as if to reach out for her, long fingers and strong hands stretching toward her in a silent plea. There was an aura around him that spoke of pain and a deep agony that made him vulnerable to darkness, but she didn't feel any evil around him, just a gray cloud of regret and guilt. And hopelessness.

It was that despair, she was certain, that called him to her in her dreams.

She needed to analyze the dreams, but life seemed to be on a whirlwind pace, leaving her with no available free time. She ignored the itch in the middle of her back, well aware that now was not the time to sneak away and take flight. Usually when she was troubled by something, she would head up to the mountains near the cabins Melissa Richter rented, but right now, Cecelia knew, was not the time to go up there. Although she could be there and back again in less than an hour, Cecelia sighed and turned back to the paperwork in front of her instead of running up the mountain.

Even though it was early, she had come down to the shop from her apartment upstairs to put away the new sheet music and unpack some of the boxes of instruments, CDs, DVDs, and other items she needed to restock the shelves of her small shop before the store opened in an hour.

Once the sheet music was displayed, she reached into the box of CDs and froze. Staring at the sexy smirk of the dark-haired rock star on the cover of the CD she held in her suddenly shaking fingers, she took a deep breath to still her rapidly beating heart.

This was *him*.

This was the man who was haunting her dreams. His face, concealed between shadow and light, now jumped out at her as if he'd always been visible. She turned the plastic case over and read the back of the Pink Melon CD.

"Brett Rhys-Falwyck. Well, hello, dream lover." She breathed out his name, surprised at how easily it rolled off her tongue. Her breath created a fog on the CD cover, temporarily covering his face in mist. His eyes bored into hers through her breath, and she shivered slightly at the unreasonable connection she felt with him.

"I hate when you do that," she whispered. Looking up as if she expected some form of response, she shook her head in resignation.

Signs were everywhere, she knew this, but this one was just a little too theatrical for her taste.

"What do you want me to do about it?" she asked softly. She looked down into the sad, tortured eyes of the man who made millions of women swoon with the sound of his voice, and shivered. Something told her they were about to meet, and that it would be sooner rather than later.

She fingered the delicate silver cross she always wore around her neck, a habit of reassuring herself it was still there. Saving souls was part of her job, and the cross was her tool for doing so. A vessel, of a sort, for capturing dying souls before the underworld did.

"Do about what, boss?"

"Oh. Hi, Glenn. Just looking at the new stock. Not sure where to put it." Cece smoothly covered her mumblings.

Glenn Johnson was a local high school senior who worked at the shop in between school, practice with his guitar (he played at the local church on Sundays and for special events), and dating. Glenn, who didn't play sports, had a quarterback's lean physique and rock star good looks, but was quiet and humble in spite of it.

"I unlocked the door," Glenn said.

"Where's Meghan?" Cece teased as she set the CD down on the counter.

"I sent her off to Coffee Haven to get us three something to drink."

Meghan Gonzalez was his newest girlfriend. She was a pretty girl who attended the local high school and was one year behind him in school. The two had been dating for a few months.

"Perfect," Cece said with a sigh. She loved coffee, something she should probably stay away from, as it was such a human beverage and she had no need to eat or drink anyway. But she loved the smell of it, and the taste of it was the closest she'd come to heaven here on earth. Her friend Sherry Grimes, girlfriend of local resident Rusty Higgins, said coffee was the nectar of the gods, and who was she to argue with that? Sherry was her dearest friend in town and was quite wise when it came to coffee.

". . . name's Brett Rhys-Falwyck, from the band, Pink Melon." Glenn was tapping the CD she'd just set down.

"Sorry," Cece apologized, "what were you saying?"

"I was saying this is the lead singer from the band Pink Melon. His name's Brett Rhys-Falwyck. Some British guy who went to school here in the States. All my friends—the female ones, that is—are gaga over him. They think he's hot. Not sure what they see in him," Glenn continued as he examined the CD cover.

Cece laughed. Glenn was pretty oblivious sometimes, so for him not to understand what was making the girls all "gaga" over this guy wasn't too surprising. To Glenn, this Brett guy was just another rocker. Girls were part of the atmosphere, he'd told her once.

Cece chuckled, ignoring Glenn's confused look.

"How about we put up the new stock? Can you handle the CDs?" she asked, covering the awkward moment with business.

Glenn nodded. Moving toward the back of the store with the box, he glanced out the window and smiled. Cece followed his gaze and saw Meghan carefully making her way to the shop with three coffees in a cardboard cup holder. Glenn hurried toward the door to open it for her. He held it for the three other customers who walked into the shop with her. Glenn was stuck holding the door and smiling for the elderly couple and young man before he could help Meghan with the coffee distribution, but his attention was immediately taken by a question from the elderly couple, whom he ushered to the appropriate section.

With a backward glance toward Meghan and Cece, he helped them find their selections. Cece was amused to see his eyes never left the front, where she and Meghan were, for more than a few seconds.

Meghan came up to the counter, smiling shyly at Cece as she

handed the store owner a cardboard cup shielded by a sleeve to protect the holder from getting burned by the hot contents. Cece accepted the cup, her fingers brushing Meghan's as she did so. Cece nearly dropped the coffee at the mental image that light touch produced.

Trying to keep her smile, Cece took a deep breath, pretending to breathe in the coffee instead of reaching out to touch Meghan again. The image was one that disturbed and alarmed Cece, but she wasn't quite sure what to make of it.

One of her abilities since coming to Havenwood Falls allowed Cece to see impressions of people—things most people preferred to keep hidden were revealed to her. But most of the images were vague and open to interpretation. In this case, the image came very clearly. Meghan was in danger.

But what kind of danger?

Cece's view had been of the girl with blood and a panicked expression on her face. Nothing else.

Meghan was wearing clothes similar to the ones she had on now, which were the usual teen attire of jeans and T-shirt and her winter jacket. Not much help in deciding when the vision would come to pass. If it even did in the way it was broadcast to her. Sometimes the visions she thought were dangerous ended up being nothing. Whatever was going to happen was going to happen soon, of that Cece was certain. What she wasn't as clear about was what she was going to do about it. She wasn't here to be involved directly with anything going on in Havenwood Falls. She was only to observe the humans, not interfere, unless specifically instructed to.

Between the visions she was having lately and the dreams of this rock star, she wasn't sure what was going on.

There was a shift in the atmosphere around the town, too. Maybe she was just acting under a heightened awareness due to her being an angel, but the goose bumps on her flesh refused to be calmed. Ever since that girl had gone missing a few months ago, she'd felt an uncomfortable weight in the air. Nothing she could put a finger on, just a feeling that something was wrong. Usually she could shake off those feelings, but not lately. The image of the rock star on the mountain briefly entered her vision and then was gone as quickly as it came, and she wasn't sure if she'd conjured him, or if his appearance in her thoughts was intentional.

Watching Meghan greet Glenn when he finally was able to join them made her smile. The two heads—hers dark, his blond—leaned together, and she heard Meghan laugh as Glenn took a sip of the hot beverage and immediately gasped as the liquid burned his tongue. The two of them grinned together as she kissed him lightly on the lips, and Glenn seemed to forget about the pain.

Perhaps I'm wrong, Cece thought. Perhaps the image was an innocent one. Perhaps she got a bloody nose, or fell and hit herself in the face. Maybe someone sent a snowball laced with ice at her. Cece made a quick sign of the cross before returning her attention to the coffee. Its strong milky-mocha scent calmed her.

Narrowing her eyes, Cece watched Meghan a few more minutes before the elderly couple approached the desk, asking for help in finding a piece of sheet music. Smiling, Cece helped them find what they were looking for before sending them out the door hand in hand, sweet smiles on their faces. She was good at that—making people feel better after being with her—and she loved being able to make folks happy.

A COUPLE HOURS LATER, Cece caught Glenn at the back of the store restocking the CDs that had been moved about by customers in the shop. He appeared deep in thought as he held the Pink Melon CD distractedly in the air, not putting it into its assigned spot marked by the plastic alphabetical tabs.

"What's up, Glenn? Something wrong?"

"No, nothing." Glenn's tone implied he was not telling her the truth.

"Want to talk about it?" Cece said gently, giving him a chance to unburden whatever was bothering him.

"I . . ." Glenn sighed and set the CD down on top of the case instead of in its slot. A sure sign that the boy, who was usually very organized and methodical, was really distressed about something.

"Meghan and I have been seeing each other for a couple of months now, you know?"

"Yep," Cece said with a grin, "I know." She couldn't help but know. The two teens were constantly smiling and touching each other.

"I really like her," Glenn confessed.

"Well, that's good . . . isn't it?"

"No, I mean . . . yes, it is good, but . . ."

"But?" Cece prompted.

"But I saw her laughing and joking with this kid at school the other day. They were talking about music, and I heard him tell her he plays the guitar and used to be in a band back home, before he moved here to Havenwood Falls."

"Oh? So you think she likes rock stars?" Cece teased.

"Yeah, I think she does." Glenn sounded so dejected that Cece took pity on him.

"Does she know you play guitar?"

"Yeah, she does, but I don't play in a band. I just play a little guitar at church, nothing as fascinating as being in a band."

Cece frowned. She really didn't want to get involved in the romance between these two teens, but Glenn looked so sad that all her instincts to heal came out and she said, "So, what do you think we can do to fix things between the two of you?"

"I don't know . . . maybe something with music that could be fun for both of us. Something kind of big that catches her attention. Like, we could invite a rock star to Havenwood Falls for a concert. Or, I know, to teach a music camp we could both go to! Maybe this guy would do it." Glenn picked up the Pink Melon CD and waved it excitedly in her face before putting it in its slot.

He walked off while Cece stood there with a slow smile spreading across her face.

A music camp! What a great lure to bring him here and maybe figure out what she was supposed to do about that darkness within him. Several days of music instruction and a workshop, a small group of students or adults working with a real rock star—that sounded pretty intriguing. Maybe they could even put on a small concert at the end of it, with songs they'd written themselves.

Hmmm, thought Cece as she stood looking at the CD, *maybe that's not such a crazy idea. I wonder how you make that happen?*

Returning to the front of the store with the CD in hand, Cece read the back cover for the information she needed and fired up her computer. After typing up a letter, she printed it, signed the bottom, slipped it into an envelope, stamped it, and put it in the basket for outgoing mail. She also sent an email just to be sure. *No sense leaving things to chance,* she thought as she hit send.

Looking up, she said, "The rest is up to you," before returning her attention to the day's receipts and shipping notifications.

NEVER SAY NEVER

(PINK MELON: ONE TIME MORE)

Written and sung by Brett Rhys-Falwyck

Never is a long time, baby
Nothing but time, baby
No matter how you long to change it
Time is gone before you know it

Never say never
Time is forever
What you wished once
can only be possible once

Opportunity doesn't always knock, baby
Sometimes you have to kick the door down, baby
Take life into your own hands
Find joy with your own hands

Never say never
Time is forever
What you wished once
can only be possible once

Don't turn your back on love, baby
Don't turn away from love, baby
There is little in this life to love
When you don't look for love

Never say never
Time is forever
What you wished once
can be possible more than once

CHAPTER 3

*B*rett rolled over, shielding his face from the sun that blinded him as it poured in from the large windows facing the ocean. He'd left them open again, and now everything felt damp and smelled of salty ocean. Sitting upright, he rubbed his face, reassured by the glance around the room that he really was back in his own bed in California and *not* lying in a field of fresh grass, watching an angel again flying off into the sunrise.

That dream had been a steady diet lately. He wished, and not for the first time, that he understood what it meant. Was he going to die? Was the angel a metaphor for his life? Did he need to set himself free?

If so, from what?

From the band? From the music that filled his life with purpose?

From thoughts of his mother and her recent death? No, that was not something he wanted to think about, not now. Not when he couldn't even remember what day of the week it was, let alone do any deep thinking about his feelings regarding his mother's death. He winced as if in pain. His mother's face swam before him.

She was smiling, but her eyes were sad. She looked disappointed. He knew she wasn't real, that her image was just a figment of his imagination, but that reality didn't make her death any easier to cope with.

He needed a drink. His mouth, dry as a bone, smelled of dead things. He reached down beside the bed and found a nearly empty bottle of champagne. Taking a long swallow, he ignored the small voice that told him this was not the way to handle his grief.

Tossing the bottle to the other side of the room, he winced when it struck the wall and rolled across the floor until resting against a chair. He shut his eyes tightly and told the voice, in a husky whisper fans wouldn't recognize, to go fuck itself.

Brett ignored the unshed tears that burned at the backs of his eyes. He knew grief could take time, but this constant ache in his heart was killing him. She wouldn't want this for him. In his mind, he knew she would want him to move on, to live his life as well as he could. But the guilt always hushed that voice. Not being there at the end was killing him inside, leaving him empty and adrift.

Brett moved, taking the sheet with him as he went, covering his naked body with it. In the bed, a lump mumbled and burrowed deeper under the cover, pulling the sheet from him even as he walked away, leaving him naked.

He glanced over, surprised to see a long slender arm reach out and disappear back under the covers. The fingers tipped with long red nails gave him no clue as to who his bed companion was. Mandy? Amanda? Mindy? He racked his brain, trying to remember whom he had invited into his bed last night.

The smell of their lovemaking lingered in the air, its musky scent mixed with salt water reminding him he needed a shower. What was that all about? He never brought anyone home. Only his bandmates had ever been inside his refuge. His life was slowly spiraling out of control, he knew it. He just didn't know how to get off the merry-go-round. And to be honest, he wasn't sure he wanted off. If he had to actually think about why he was acting this way, he would have to remember the reason for the pain and guilt. He didn't want to do that.

Every day he woke unaware of where he was or what he was doing. He was lost in an ocean of indecision and choices, none of which he felt prepared to make.

Thank God I don't do drugs, he thought, *or this could be really bad.*

As the water coursed over his toned body, he leaned against the cool wall of the shower and let the tears flow. Salt mingled with the warm water and shampoo. So lost in thought was he that he nearly jumped out of his skin when he felt fingers sliding down his back, followed by the pressure of a body pressing against him. Her form was as cool and soothing as her fingers.

"Hello, big boy," she purred, turning him around to face her.

Steam surrounded them, shrouding her face in shadows that ebbed and flowed around her, obscuring everything but a vague estimation of her form. He was distracted by her hands, which were sliding up his chest to the back of his neck, pulling his face down to hers, where she hungrily pulled his tongue inside her moist mouth. He grabbed her hair, and long blond tresses wrapped around his hands as he held her captive, finding that he couldn't get enough of the taste of her.

His body reacted, and he pulled her closer, still not sure whom he was caressing until she whispered against his lips that the bed might be more comfortable, and he realized this must be his lover from the night before.

With that, she slipped from the steam-filled shower and was gone before he even opened his eyes.

Turning off the water, he grabbed a towel and knotted it around his middle. When he padded into the bedroom, a silly grin on his face, he found his bed partner still sleeping in the same position he'd left her just moments ago.

Twisting back to look at the shower, he watched as the petite footsteps of the ghost lover disappeared in front of his eyes as if they'd never been there. Turning back to the woman in the bed, he shook his head to clear it. How was that possible? The footsteps were going away from the bed and toward the door to the deck. He followed them outside, but there was no one there, and then the prints vanished. What was going on? He looked over his shoulder at the bed.

The covers had slipped from the sleeping form just enough to reveal auburn hair spilling down the side of the mattress to just above the carpet. This was not the woman who'd been in the shower with him. Rubbing his face in confusion, he wondered, *what the hell? Who was I just kissing?*

BRETT BREATHED A SIGH OF RELIEF. Amanda, the girl who'd shared his bed last night, had finally left with a few giggles and thanks for a great night and hints that she wouldn't mind doing it again. Brett smiled, let her cling to him while they waited for the Uber driver to arrive, and then escorted her to the car with no firm promises.

He paid the Uber driver double the fee to keep his address a secret, then went back inside his house, his thoughts already on his next problem—trying to figure out what happened in the shower that morning.

The woman in the shower had felt so real, so warm, and so solid in his arms. She'd fit into his embrace like she'd been there before. Her kiss—his hand went to his lips, fingers tracing where she'd pressed her own to him so firmly—still resonated in his mind. His heart raced once more just thinking about her. He couldn't imagine what would happen if he ever actually held her. On second, thought, judging by the way his body immediately reacted, he was pretty sure he did know what would happen if she were ever really in his arms.

She'd tasted sweet and salty all at the same time. Like an ocean wave, she'd bowled him over, leaving him gasping for air. And yet, he couldn't have kissed her, the woman of his dreams. The only woman who'd been in his house had been Amanda, a redhead, not a blonde. Unless it had been some kind of wet dream that had manifested itself into reality, the encounter in the shower never happened. *Right? Never happened. Yep, that's my story, and I'm sticking to it,* Brett thought. But the way his body still craved her belied his protests.

An hour later, he was still pondering this encounter when his doorbell rang. He let the noise echo, not moving from his seated position on the deck overlooking the ocean. He was fascinated by the waves, their ebb and flow pulling sand and stone and sea debris out to sea, or depositing it back on the shore. He was remembering beach trips with his mother when he was a little boy. He'd had a bright red pail and a yellow shovel and one of those sifter things that went with him every time they'd managed a few hours in the sun.

Running against the waves had been his favorite summer activity. That and splashing his mom, who'd squeal with feigned annoyance at his antics, and then hug him until they both were laughing so hard, they couldn't stand up and would collapse into the sand just as a big wave came up to splash the gritty material from their bodies. He remembered the tug of the waves as they tried to pull him from his mother and how she'd hold onto him, wiping his tears with a salty hand as she promised him she'd never leave, would always be there for him.

He took a swallow of his tea, then leaned his head back, letting the sun hit him full in the face, its warmth making a mockery of the coldness in his heart that was all he felt these days. The sound of the ocean was its own rhythm. Gentle and relentless, it roared in his mind like an oncoming train. He couldn't get off the tracks, knew the train was going to run him over, and even though it was only metaphorical, he wanted it to end his pain. Between worry about the band, the upcoming Grammy Award show appearance, the weird dreams he was having lately, and his mother's death, Brett didn't think he had it in him anymore to get up out of the chair. He just wanted to stay there and not think, but the thoughts wouldn't stay away.

The ocean was soothing with its endless and repetitive comings and goings, yet he could find no comfort in it anymore. Every day it was there to greet him, stormy gray or robin's egg blue, depending on its mood. The ocean never apologized, never sought to be anything it wasn't. The ocean was always the same, and yet ever-changing.

Just like he was.

He took another sip of his tea, wincing at the coldness of it. This was his third cup, and each one had gone cold while he stared from his deck out to the ocean. He set the cup down on the deck floor next to his chair and sighed deeply, the kind of sigh that took all his breath.

"Are you aware you have exactly one hour before the car comes to pick you up for the airport so we can fly off to our mother-effin' *Grammy appearance*? I bet you haven't even packed yet, have you?"

"Cooly," Brett said flatly. Standing up, Brett stretched and then leaned down to pick up the cup he'd set on the floor.

"Brett, I've been trying to call you. You aren't answering your phone these days?" When Brett ignored him, Cooly continued. "First, we gotta get you ready to go, and then we gotta talk.

Cooly pointed toward the door leading back inside.

With a final glance toward the ocean, sun sparkling on the tips of the waves turning them a rosy gold, Brett followed Cooly into the cool interior of the house. In the kitchen, Brett offered tea or coffee to his friend, but Cooly turned them both down, opting instead for a beer from the fridge. Popping off the top, he downed the Heineken in three swallows, then reached for a second beer.

"Slow down there, cowboy," Brett said with a chuckle. "You aren't planning to drive when you leave, are you?"

Cooly took a slow swallow and set the beer down. Wiping his mouth, he turned and looked at Brett with an expression of such sadness that Brett's breath caught on his next words.

"What's going on with you these days, man? If I'd known the band taking a break was going to hit you this hard, I would've waited until after the Grammys to bring it up."

Brett sighed. He didn't want to talk about it. Walking toward the fridge, he reached inside and pulled out a beer for both of them. They drank in silence.

Brett finally said, "I just have a lot to think about these days. I'm trying to work through some things."

"We all do, man." Cooly placed the half-drunk beer on the counter. Looking at his phone, he said, "We have about forty-five minutes before the cab gets here. Go take a shower and pack your bags. Get the gear you need. We'll talk more on the plane."

Brett nodded. He knew his friend was right—he needed to focus on priorities.

"Yeah, okay. You're right," he said.

"Whatever happened to that ski trip you were talking about taking?"

Brett shook his head, "Nothing happened. I was just joking. Funny thing, though, I got a brochure from that place."

He waved his hand toward the counter where his mail had piled up, unopened and unlooked at. The brochure for Havenwood Falls was on top of the pile, along with a letter.

"What's this?" Cooly held up the envelope.

Brett looked at the envelope, frowning slightly. "Not sure, looks pretty thick though."

He opened the letter and whistled as he scanned the contents.

There were several pages, and he set a couple of them back on the counter as he read the top one. "Well, this is interesting."

"What is?" Cooly asked. Moving to stand beside Brett, he read over his shoulder.

"This letter is from someone in Havenwood Falls, asking me to come and run a short music camp. They will take care of transportation," he nodded toward one of the other pages, "and provide lodging as well."

"Now that is interesting," agreed Cooly. "Think you'll go?"

"I will think about it," Brett said. He stuffed the pages back in the envelope and folded it carefully before putting it in the pocket of his jeans. "Guess I need to get ready. Help me?"

Cooly nodded and followed his friend. Clapping a hand on Brett's shoulder he said, "I think some time away might be good for you."

Brett nodded in agreement, not saying anything. It felt good to have his friend by his side. He hadn't realized how much he'd missed him until now.

OCEAN OF OUR LOVE

(BRETT RHYS-FALWYCK SOLO ALBUM: OCEANS)

Written and sung by Brett Rhys-Falwyck

The ocean of your love comes in on waves of emotion
that nearly drag me under
Like the uncertainty of my heart
you conceal your true intention

The movement of your endless sea
is a rhythm unlike any other
It calls to me with a siren's song
irresistible and urgent

You are my wild ocean
and I your waiting shore
breathless for your salty kisses
always wanting more and more

The movement of your ocean
is a rhythm unlike any other
It calls to me with a siren's song
irresistible and urgent

You are the message in the bottle
bouncing at the whim of the current
bringing hope to the broken
your love a deterrent

The movement of your ocean
is a rhythm unlike any other
It calls to me with a siren's song
irresistible and urgent

I will wait for you, my little mermaid
until the sand becomes my grave
My song and your song
will echo across the waves

CHAPTER 4

"Glenn, everything put away?"

Nodding, Glenn greeted a few customers and friends from school who wandered in and out of the store as he made his way toward her.

"Do you need something, boss?" he asked. He was standing on the other side of the counter from her. Looking over his shoulder at the clock, she saw he had another half hour of his shift left.

Outside the window, she'd noticed a couple of girls hanging around, giggling and pointing at him as he worked. They didn't come in, and she wondered why, feeling it had something to do with Meghan, who was also in the store most of the day.

Even though Meghan and Glenn had held a few hushed conversations, Cece hadn't noticed anything amiss between the teens. She wondered if Glenn's fears about Meghan being interested in the new kid at school were groundless, but she did notice how the girl watched the people who'd come in to use the recording studio in the back as if she was waiting for someone.

Did Meghan's eyes linger a little longer than necessary on the guys with guitars, or was Cece just imagining it based on Glenn's fears? Cece wished she had a better grasp on teenagers' hormones, because from what she could see, Meghan didn't appear to spend any time talking to anyone but Glenn.

Meghan had grabbed one of the small tables at the back of the store where customers could sit and enjoy coffee while friends used the small recording studio. Cece had built the studio so local musicians could record demo tapes, and residents could make special messages for their friends' anniversaries, birthdays, and other occasions. The booth was very popular with some of the teens in town who liked to hear themselves play and sing. Some of the kids were pretty good, while others were quite enthusiastic, which she supposed made up for their lack of real talent.

In the back of the store, right outside the studio, Cece had set up three small round tables, scratched and dented from long-term use, along with several chairs at each table. There was a single-cup coffee maker with assorted teas, coffees, and hot chocolate available for customers. She also kept a supply of cookies on hand from the town's bakery.

The store offered free Wi-Fi, which meant the tables were usually occupied most of the day, but she had a strict policy of not allowing anyone to sit there for more than a couple of hours at a time. Her store was small, but did a steady business.

She'd been here about three years now, and loved Havenwood Falls with a passion that surprised her. She contributed to the town's sports teams and the local high school band program when asked to sponsor trips or other fundraisers, but she didn't go out of her way to be involved in any particular activity. She hadn't joined any committees in town, but had been a large contributor to the fund to rebuild the library after the disastrous fire.

She loved, and often frequented, Howe's Herbal Shoppe and sometimes visited with Sherry and Rusty. For the most part, though, Cece tried to stay to herself.

She had regular customers, and her shop was even a spot the

tourists liked to visit, but even as steady as her business was, she was always looking for new ways to bring in more and to help students, who were her biggest customers. She enjoyed being around young people. Their energy revitalized her and gave her a fresh perspective on the human condition.

Heading to the back of the shop, she nearly stumbled as she felt a sudden lightheadedness. Grabbing onto the edge of one of the tables, she steadied herself for a moment, then shook herself free of the feeling before clasping her hand over her necklace. Reassured it was still there, she continued on into the studio. She needed to do her daily equipment check. She sat in the swivel chair and played with a few of the buttons on the sound machine to make sure everything was working properly. Looking under the desk, she felt the lightheadedness return and closed her eyes.

Water, pounding. Glass, slick with steam. A man. His body hard against hers. Twisting to keep her wing nubs inside and away from prying hands, she leaned into the kiss. His mouth was firm and yet soft. Playfully she invited him back to bed . . .

"What the hell . . . ?" Cece stood up, her body shivering with emotion unlike anything she'd felt before.

"Boss, you okay?" Glenn stood at the door to the studio, looking at her with concern.

"Yesss . . ." Cece said shakily. Taking a deep breath, she strode past Glenn without another word. She needed air. Desperately needed air.

Stepping outside the shop, she took a deep breath. The two girls who'd been standing nearby glanced at her with curiosity before walking away, whispering to each other as they left. Cece ignored them, focusing instead on getting her breathing back to normal. Deeply inhaling the cool, crisp air, she regained control of her body.

What was happening? Why was this man, someone she'd never met, so much a part of her thoughts these days?

It was the sadness in his eyes that drew her to him, of that she was certain. Wrapping her hand in her ponytail, she tugged, the pain of pulling her hair bringing her back to the present.

He touched me there, she thought, dropping her hands and letting her hair fall. *And I liked it.*

Reaching for the door handle, she heard a voice, drifting past her on the wind, say, *Bring him here.*

Goosebumps rising on her flesh, she closed her eyes, waiting for more, but the voice said nothing else. She didn't need to ask who needed to come. She already knew who it was.

"I'm trying," she whispered. "But why?"

Her only answer was a growing feeling of urgency.

BRETT HATED FLYING. The flight was uneventful except for a little turbulence just before they landed that caused a momentary panic in him. Harry and Sticks were wound up, chatting incessantly and signing autographs every time they were asked. They were enjoying the hoopla that came with being in a successful band much more than he was. Cooly watched him with concern, but didn't say anything, and for that Brett was grateful. He wasn't in the mood to talk about anything right now.

The band was up for Best Pop Duo/Group Performance and Song of the Year for "Love Is Like a Memory," and Brett was up for an individual award for writing the song that had catapulted the band to fame. The connecting flight was filled with other celebrities, and selfies were being taken everywhere. Brett stayed out of the chaos as best he could, but managed to get his face into several of the backgrounds of other pictures being posted all over social media.

Nodding and smiling, he kept pretty much to himself. As soon as he sat down, he plugged in his headphones and turned the music up loudly on his latest playlist. Flying was not something he enjoyed, and any way he could find to ignore the fact that he was in a tin can moving at speeds he couldn't even fathom across the skies high above the very hard ground, the happier he was.

As a matter of fact—and this was not something he was proud of—his fear of flying was part of what had kept him from getting to his mother until after she passed. He couldn't forgive himself for that lack of familial responsibility. He'd sent money, he'd called, but when she really needed him, he'd failed her.

Wincing at the memory, he put his head down, turned up the volume on his iPod, and tried to ignore the crowds of fans and celebrities around him, which was not easy, since even other celebrities had heard their music and wanted to congratulate him on the band's success.

He was gracious but cool, not inviting conversation or further closeness, and after a while, everyone got the hint and left him alone. Leaning back, he'd just closed his eyes when the flight attendant came by with the drink cart. He woke at the gentle nudge of the elderly woman seated beside him and requested a whiskey on the rocks. He handed the stewardess his credit card and downed the drink in one gulp.

She handed him his card back, along with a meal.

Putting the tray down, Brett reached for his salad just as turbulence sent the meal sailing out of his hands to land in the lap of the woman seated behind him. A squeal told him she wasn't too pleased about that, and he unbuckled his belt to lean over the seat and apologize. Her head was bent forward as she plucked salad and croutons from her lap. Blond hair fell in a curtain around her, and for a second, Brett was left speechless. This was the woman he'd been dreaming of—but no, once she raised her head, he realized that was not the case.

Apologizing once more, he accepted his half container of salad and retook his seat. Heart pounding, he was left to wonder at his overreaction. Was he going to act like this around every petite blond woman he met?

Get control of yourself, buddy. You'll have a heart attack if you keep reacting like this.

"Brett, you okay?" Cooly asked. Brett could see the concern on his friend's face. Glancing up, Brett nodded as he swallowed a mouth full of salad.

"Yeah, I'm cool. How about you?"

"You know me. I'm the coolest of the cool. After all, my name is Cooly," his friend repeated the familiar joke.

Both men laughed half-heartedly without any real mirth, and Cooly moved on to the back of the plane.

Brett finished the salad, barely tasting it. His thoughts kept returning to his reaction toward the woman into whose lap his salad had fallen. His heart had finally stopped pounding, but his mind couldn't stay away from the image of the ghost who haunted his dreams, and now his showers, too.

Who was she? Why was she in his thoughts all the time now, when he'd never seen her before?

Nothing to worry about. You're not going mad, he reassured himself.

Brett gazed out the window at a sky filled with large white puffy clouds in an endless sea of blue. Below, the ground was barely visible, just green or brown shapes broken by the gray ribbons of roads and the shiny silver of rivers and lakes. His salad finished, he yawned. Lowering the small flap over the window and cutting out the view, he leaned back, closing his eyes and shifting until he was comfortable.

In seconds, he was asleep and snoring slightly.

∾

BRETT OPENED *his eyes to the sound of birds chirping and the constant buzz of insects. A gentle breeze floated by, ruffling his hair, its temperature just slightly below that of the sun-filled glade, causing him to shiver. His back was against the reassuring solidness of the large rock he usually found himself near. He stretched his arms overhead, wiggling his bottom until he was comfortable.*

The sun was warm like just-harvested honey, its rich color painting everything around him with an amber-hued glow. He sighed in contentment. This was home to him, familiar and safe.

The smell of pine was subtle and tickled his nose with its astringent odor. It was both pleasant and unpleasant at the same time. He glanced around, taking in the way the grass undulated in the breeze, and the graceful swaying of the bright yellow flowers on their stalks.

He heard the subtle music of that glade with a musician's ear, and appreciated the symphony with a small smile that relaxed him.

Here was peace.

Here was serenity.

Eyes closing against the sun's warmth and with a contented sigh, he slipped into slumber. A rustling, discordant in its randomness, woke him. Sitting upright, he shook the sandman from his eyes and followed the sound that disturbed his rest until he observed a woman bathed in a white light that nearly blinded him. Partially covering his eyes with one raised hand, he tried to get a good look at her, but the light prevented a clear view.

"Who are you?" his dream self asked her, but she didn't answer. Instead, she opened her arms as if to embrace him before falling, her white dress billowing around her, over the nearby cliff's edge.

He jumped upright, intent on saving her, but instead, he found himself eye to eye with an angel of such beauty that he cried out in shock and desire. Reaching for her, his hand gripped only air as the angel flew away without a backward glance, leaving him precariously perched on the edge of the cliff she'd just leapt from.

He cried out once more, angry and desolate without her. He watched as she disappeared into the sun as if she was heading home, her beautiful form swallowed into the golden orb and lost to view.

Tears, hot and wet, slid down his cheeks.

"I DON'T KNOW who she is, but if you don't stay on your side of the seat, you're gonna regret it."

Brett woke to find himself curling up against the elderly woman next to him as if they were spooning. Appalled, he quickly moved away, apologizing. But the annoyed woman, once he was in his own space, ignored him, muttering under her breath, "Next time I'm asking for the seat NOT next to the drunk, drugged-out rock star."

She glared darkly at Brett before returning to her book.

"I'm not . . . Oh, whatever," Brett said, the protest that he was not a drunk, drugged-out rock star dying on his lips. What did it matter, anyway?

They disembarked from the plane a few hours later, and Brett retrieved his suitcase and guitar with the rest of the band. Harry and Sticks hadn't stopped talking the whole trip and were really hyped up by the time they arrived at their hotel.

Brett immediately went to the bathroom for a shower in preparation for their trip to the venue to test out their equipment, do a sound check, and prepare for their performance later that night. They were due to be picked up in about an hour and would have about an hour and a half to make sure everything was in order for their performance. Most of the other bands and singers had arrived the day before, but Pink Melon had not been scheduled to travel until today, due to their busy schedule.

They would be singing just the one song, the one they hoped would rocket them further up the ladder to stardom, but after the bombshell dropped by Cooly, Brett had a feeling it would land them on the list of one-hit wonders.

Leaning against the shower wall, hot water streaming down his naked back, he flexed his muscles and tried not to cry. The band's breaking up wasn't a bad thing. He had a feeling they were going in different directions anyway, but they'd only just cut their first album, and breaking out with this song, he worried what he'd be doing next.

Back to studio musician?

Backup in another band?

Start another band?

He owned the rights to the songs he'd written, only having to pay residuals to the other band members if he used the songs he'd written while with this band, so he could continue to write songs and make his living that way.

Or he could go solo. He could do it—play small venues like colleges and small concert halls, or play with symphonies until he got his name out there again as a solo artist.

But even as he thought it, he wasn't sure that would work for him. He liked the comfort of being in a band, having a bunch of people he could rely on to distract him when things grew too dark in his mind.

You probably couldn't do it on your own, anyway, the dark voice whispered into his mind.

Turning off the water and wiping his hand down his toned, taut chest to remove excess soap, he shrugged. *I don't have to decide right now. Let's just get through tonight,* he consoled himself. *Then we can worry about the ten-year plan.*

"Brett, come on, man. Are you done yet? The rest of us gotta get pretty too, you know." Brett chuckled at Harry's comment.

"Gonna take more than soap and water to pretty you up, man," he shouted back through the door as he took a final glance at himself in the mirror. Other than the bags under his eyes from not enough sleep, he guessed he was presentable.

Slipping a towel around his middle, he unlocked the door and stepped out. The other three were standing around, nibbling on the snacks the hotel had provided for them as special guests of the event. They all turned to stare at him when he joined them.

"You okay?" Cooly asked. He wore the same worried expression he'd had while they were on the plane.

"Yeah, I'm fine. Why? Do I look that bad?" Brett countered, putting Cooly on the spot, then instantly regretting the adversarial attitude. He softened his expression, slapping his buddy on the back and reiterating, "Really. I'm fine."

"Okay, if you say so," his friend responded with an arched brow that indicated he didn't believe him. Turning to the other band members, Cooly said, "Who wants the shower next?"

"Should we maybe take a minute to talk about stuff?" Harry asked. "We kind of left things up in the air and I just . . . Well, I wondered if we needed to maybe talk about where we are before we go on stage tonight?"

Brett shook his head, holding a palm out to stop the conversation in its tracks. "Can we wait until after the show tonight? We have enough stress as it is. Why add to it?"

They glanced at each other, looking relieved. He could tell by the way they nodded their heads so readily that they were dreading this conversation as much as he was. It could wait. Anything earth-shattering needed to be said when they could all give it their full attention, not when they were rushing out to a performance.

Heading toward his room off the center suite, Brett closed the door and dressed as quickly as he could. He still laid his clothes out like he used to when he was a schoolboy, and today was no different.

Boots, black with white lacing, size ten; socks, dark with his favorite skull pattern on them in a bright white, a gift last Christmas from Cooly; pants—designer black skinny jeans that hugged his body, but were stretchy enough to allow him to do his gyrations without fear of splitting them; underwear, nothing fancy there, just plain white; the shirt was one he'd agonized over for quite a while before finally packing a soft black denim shirt with a long black fringe on the inside of the sleeves that looked like dark angel wings when he lifted his arms; and finally, the bandana. He looked at the bandana—a dark navy with white skulls on it—and decided he wouldn't wear it tonight. He would let his hair float freely on stage, but he tucked it in his pocket in case he changed his mind. He decided to forgo the black leather vest he usually wore, so nothing would interfere with the winged effect of the fringe.

Brett took an extra minute to check his appearance in the mirror. He ran his hand over his unshaven jaw that was dusted with dark stubble, hesitating. Stubble was sexy, at least that's what the women all said. Besides, it leant him an air of mysteriousness that suited his dark mood.

Stepping out of the room, he found his bandmates waiting for him by the door.

"Ready?" asked Cooly.

"Ready, able, and willing," said Sticks, and with a grand gesture like Vanna turning a letter, he bowed, motioning for them all to exit the room ahead of him.

Brett turned to look at the suite before he closed the door behind them, and sighed. They were about to step out onto a stage they'd been dreaming of their whole lives, and it might be their first and last time ever doing it as a band. Staring at his friends with speculation, he realized he would miss them all if that were the case. They may not be of the same blood, but they were brothers all the same.

He wasn't sure he was ready to close this chapter of his life, not with so many others already closing or closed, but he wasn't sure what other option he had. The band had been formed by them as a group, so the decision to end it would have to be a group decision as well. At least they were giving him that courtesy.

They walked through the lobby downstairs and out to their

waiting limo without stopping for interviews or autographs, each of them dealing with fame and the upcoming performance in their own way.

Brett's game face consisted of a stern expression, focused eyes, and a muscle that twitched in his jaw every few minutes. Beside him, he felt Cooly's breathing relax as they settled into the limo, away from the chaos of fame. Their guitars and other instruments had already been sent to the venue, and Brett felt oddly naked without his guitar bag in his hand.

"Anyone else here forgotten the words to all the songs?" Harry's comment got them all talking again in a rush of noise and laughter, and Brett thought, *There's no place I would rather be right at this moment.*

FALLING

(BRETT RHYS-FALWYCK SOLO ALBUM: OCEANS)

Written and sung by Brett Rhys-Falwyck

I stand atop the world,
my arms open wide
A titanic range of emotions
take me on a wild ride

Nothing can hold me back
more than the arms that hold me close
Don't drop me
I'm falling . . .
. . . falling
. . . falling

My heart beats a frantic rhythm
holding onto the emotion
that throws me overboard
in a sea of constant motion

Nothing can hold me back
more than the arms that hold me close
Don't drop me
I'm falling . . .
. . . falling
. . . falling

Winged, I soar battered and bruised
into a storm of crows
They beat me back with black knives
and cry out, we know, we know

Nothing can hold me back
more than the arms that hold me close
Don't drop me
I'm falling . . .
. . . falling
. . . falling

CHAPTER 5

*I*n spite of Harry's fears, nobody forgot all the words. The sound check went well. Quite a few of the crew working behind the scenes, and the other celebrities passing by, stopped to listen and watch them perform.

Brett ignored them all as he struggled to get the words to sound right. He felt like he was walking in molasses every time he tried to take a step. The energy was draining out of him. Maybe he was tired from the flight? Or maybe the weight of the world had finally caught up to him. Whatever the problem was, he knew he had to shake it off before their performance. Straightening his shoulders, he slid his fingers down the guitar for emphasis and began again, letting the music swell inside him like it always did.

Brett had a rule, and he was glad to see that the bright lights of fame hadn't made his bandmates forget that every performance was *the* performance. So even if they were doing a sound check or just playing for a few friends, they did every show as if it was the show people were paying for. They all played and sang their hearts out, leaving everything on the stage for the crew to mop up after them.

When the last chord had twanged into silence, the people

watching and listening gave them a standing ovation and slaps on the back as they walked off stage.

"That was awesome, man," said an old rocker Brett remembered his mom saying she listened to as a kid. This old man still had an ear for good music, and Brett perked up like a peacock on hearing the man's praise.

A few hours later, Brett and the other members of the band, nervously pacing around the venue as it filled with audience members and other musicians, went backstage to check on their equipment and confirm the time of their appearance. They were actually moved up to first to perform, right before the presentation of the first award they were nominated for, and Brett was stoked about the order.

Originally, they'd been scheduled to perform in the third spot, but maybe their sound check performance had impressed the organizers enough that they decided to put Pink Melon in the coveted first performance time slot.

Brett could see the first presenters taking their places in the wings on the other side of the stage. The house lights dimmed. The emcee, an actor of some note, stepped up to the front of the stage and began his monologue. The audience laughed, but Brett barely heard. He ran through the words to the song as he tried to keep from giving in to his nerves. Stretching his fingers, imagining the chords and their positioning on the guitar, he relaxed. He slowed his breathing, letting the atmosphere weave around him, feeding his desire to be in front of his peers, playing a song he loved. His mother's image, clouded with a dusty gold hue, rose up in his mind.

She was smiling, nodding to him, her eyes full of love. Then her form disappeared.

He saw the mountain, and the younger woman appeared in view. Her slight form was shrouded in a silvery light that highlighted her perfectly muscled arms. This time she was wearing a long white gown that lightly brushed across the top of the grass, her steps so light she appeared to be floating, and he realized her wings were in full view even if her face wasn't. She turned, head lowered so her golden hair curtained her face, and he couldn't see more than a soft cheek and sharp jaw before the image faded into memory as reality interrupted the vision.

Opening his eyes, he looked out from the curtained area backstage where he stood with the crew. Next to him, a man held a clipboard and talked softly into a small microphone running along his jawline.

Brett nodded to him, shrugging his shoulders in apology. He'd missed his chance to take his assigned seat and was stuck here for a bit. Intrigued by what was happening out on the stage, Brett watched the show unfolding. From this vantage point, he could see just how the show was put together, and it was a marvel of logistics and coordination that defied reason. How did everyone know where to go, and how to get there, without bumping into each other? He silently applauded their efficiency as all the bits and pieces of the show moved together with seamless precision.

The emcee on stage introduced the presenters, who confidently strode across the stage from the side opposite Brett's position. The girl floated to her assigned spot in a beautiful red ball gown, which she navigated with grace and no trips. He had to give her a lot of credit for that, because to him, that dress looked like a nightmare to walk in. She was on the arm of a very tall, thin actor whom he remembered seeing in a couple films, but his nervousness made his mind blank on the name.

Brett took a deep breath, wishing it would quiet his nerves, but not holding out much hope. Nervousness was the least of his problems. Worry over his performance had him closing his eyes just as a photographer standing backstage came up to where he stood, snapping some candid shots. Brett waited for the cue to walk on stage.

Brett opened his eyes just as the photographer moved past in the semi-darkness. They nodded to each other, and Brett heard the click of the man's camera but thought nothing of it. After a while, the activity that went on around them just became noise without meaning.

On stage, the emcee cracked a few jokes about the category that had everyone laughing. The cameras panned over the audience, lingering on a few of the more famous celebrities.

Pink Melon's instruments and equipment were being moved closer to the stage, ready to be placed on the small raised dais just out of sight of the audience, as it was concealed behind the curtains. Out of the way, but close to the stage, Brett could see their guitars and drums twinkling a bit in the dim light, and he breathed deeply to still his pounding heart. It was nearly time. They were about to catapult to the fame they'd always wanted. Why, then, did he feel like he was drowning?

Pacing in the darkness backstage, Brett nearly bumped into his manager, Graham Locke, whom he hadn't seen in months.

"Hey, Brett, my man, may I have a few words with you?" Graham appeared nervous, and his left eye was twitching, a sure sign he was about to deliver bad news.

"Well, well, if it ain't Lucky Locke, our manager," said Cooly, coming up between Brett and their manager. "Where have you been hiding?"

"Hiding?" The effect of Lucky's indignant tone was spoiled by his slurred words as he focused on the one part of Cooly's comments he could answer. Nothing is more pitiful than a whiny drunk, and Lucky was all of that and more. *Especially tonight*, thought Brett with a bit of worry starting a headache between his eyes.

Brett and Cooly exchanged a glance. On a night as important as this, they didn't need their manager making a scene.

Locke licked his lips, avoiding Cooly's gaze with practiced ease. "Just here to chat with Brett, that's all. I just need a word . . ."

Brett could smell the alcohol on the older man's breath as he turned his back to Cooly and faced Brett. Locke looked like he needed a quick shower and some sobering up. Now was not the time to be dealing with this. Brett looked to Cooly for help.

This wasn't the first time their manager had shown up before a performance in this condition. Brett wanted Locke gone. The emcee was about to introduce them.

Lucky Locke was an undeserved nickname, one that the man had earned for exactly the opposite reason than what one would think his name implied. The name fit him like "Tiny" did a Sumo wrestler in his prime.

Pink Melon had signed with Lucky when the band first got together. Lucky was some kind of relation to a former girlfriend of one of the band members, and he caught them when they were pretty green and hungry for success. He talked a good game, convincing them he knew what he was doing and would take them to the pinnacles of success. Since then, the band had had to bail him out of jail more times than any of them could count, and any attempts to remove him from their management team had been unsuccessful. As good as he might be at losing money, he was a pro at creating iron-clad contracts, and theirs was no exception. They couldn't let him go unless he wanted to go. And with the gravy train they turned out to be, his leaving them appeared to be an impossibility.

Brett and Cooly had tried to get the contract voided due to Lucky's financial woes, but all the outside bookkeepers they hired could find nothing wrong with the books. Other than busting up the band and everyone disappearing for a couple of years, there was no way to get out of the contract. They were stuck with him.

"What do you need, Lucky?" Brett said, stepping out of the other man's embrace. "We're about to go on stage. If you have something to say, then say it."

"Yesh, I know that," Lucky said, his words slurring more and more as he talked. Brett wondered how much he'd already imbibed, and prayed the old man wouldn't vomit on him. That had happened before, and it wasn't pretty.

"Lost it . . . all. I losht it . . . all . . . ," said Lucky with a blubbering wail at the end of his almost undecipherable statement.

"Lost all what?" asked Brett, not fully understanding what the manager was trying to tell him. Lucky kept trying to get Brett in a death hold, but Brett easily stepped away from him, waving a hand between them to keep from gagging on Lucky's alcohol-sodden breath.

Brett pushed Lucky away, but the manager wasn't so easily distracted. Clinging to Brett's arm, he refused to let go. Brett looked back into the wings and was relieved to see one of the security guards move closer and pull Lucky away.

"Ready?" The guy with the clipboard and the headphones looked at them with a bored expression. Holding the headphones tight against his ear for a moment as the stage went dark, he whispered into the mouthpiece for the crew to move the instruments to the stage. Nodding to Brett and the band, he gestured them forward.

Brett looked at his bandmates and smiled. "No matter what happens in the future, tonight is the night we shine, got it?"

His voice was confident, his steps more so. He could only hope the butterflies inside his stomach were also aware he was in control.

As they took their positions, Brett lifted his guitar over his head, flashing toned abs as he did so, causing a few squeals of appreciation from the female members of the audience in front of them who could just see the band in the dim light.

When the spotlight hit him, it was a bit of a shock, and Brett took a deep breath before breaking into song. Once his fingers hit the opening chords, Brett felt transformed into the song, with a deep connection to the words. He played like his life depended on it, the darkness slipping away in the bright lights and hopeful words.

Moving forward, his mouth so close to the microphone every woman in the audience wished she were the amplifier, he sang. Breathing out the words, his fingers striking the chords and holding them for full effect, he played without even realizing the other members of the band were there with him.

The audience rose to their feet as the song's last chord echoed. Shouts and whistles—the kind you gave to a team that just won an important sporting event—rang out, and the emcee had a hard time getting the audience to quiet down.

Taking a quick bow, each member blew a kiss to the audience in gratitude before stepping into the darkness backstage. The crew was on the stage to set up the next band almost before the last Pink Melon band member entered the curtains offstage. Brett held his guitar loosely in his hand as he made his way toward the room they were using for storage.

"May I take that for you, sir?" asked one of the crew. He gestured toward the guitar, and Brett handed it over without a second thought.

"If you'll follow the fellow in the red jacket, he'll take you to your seats in time for the announcement of the winners of the category you are nominated in. You will need to hurry."

Brett and the others followed the usher. He held out the small penlight toward the stairs that led to the main floor. Once they reached the stairs another usher led them to their assigned seats. They were in the middle of the row, of course, so had to apologize several times as they made their way past their idols before settling in their seats. The house lights returned to normal as the commercial break ended.

The emcee made a comment about the band, and Brett grinned widely. Turning, he saw the same expression on the faces of Cooly, Harry, and Sticks. They all wiped their foreheads like they'd just survived something momentous, which they had, of course. Later, when they saw the video replay of their gestures, they would groan at the cheesiness of that decision, but not apologize for it. The emcee introduced the two singers who would announce the nominees for Best Pop Duo/Group Performance.

Brett found his attention wandering as he looked around. The butterflies had returned. He felt overwhelmed and small in this room of famous, and infamous, musicians. Some he'd looked up to since childhood, some he'd emulated with his own playing, and some he was so awed at seeing, he could feel his breath catch in his throat as he thought how lucky he was to be here. Judging by the starstruck looks on the faces of his friends, they were equally shocked to be here among their idols.

His attention snapped back to the stage when he heard his band's name announced with the list of other nominees.

"Pink Melon. I like those guys," the girl said with a giggle as she took the card from the male announcer and tore it open.

Giggling again, she quipped, "And the winner is . . ."

Brett held his breath, waiting for the words he both dreaded and longed to hear.

The male presenter peered over her shoulder and finished the announcement with, "Pink Melon! Come on up, you guys, and claim your prize. Look at that, I'm a poet."

"And I bet ya didn't know it," the female said with another giggle.

Cooly, Harry, and Sticks held hands while raising their arms up high in a victory salute as they accepted the award from the statuesque models who were handing them out. Brett, walking across the stage with a slow, measured gait, reached them just as Cooly leaned in toward the microphone to give thanks for the award and to list the people who deserved credit for the band's success, then he stepped aside to let Brett have his say.

Brett stepped up to the microphone for his moment. Tossing

his hair back, he looked directly into the camera and said as the music to cut off their speeches began to play, "Give me a minute, guys, this is important."

To his surprise, the music stopped. Brett held up the award and stared at it for a few seconds as he gathered his thoughts.

"The guys and I want you to know that Pink Melon is not a fly-by-night band. We're not a one-hit wonder. We are here to stay. We'll be back on this stage again, God willing, and with your help, other dreams will come true. I want to take a moment to thank my mom, who recently passed away. She was a great woman who always encouraged me to do my best, and I want to pass that advice on to all of you. Do your best, and the best will happen for you, too. That's all. You can start the music again, folks. We're done."

Cooly met Brett's eyes before sliding his glance toward the other two, who also looked a bit chastened by Brett's speech. They all three turned to look back at Brett. The four grabbed hands, putting them up in the air as a sign of solidarity that Brett hoped rang literally true before going backstage.

"Mr. Falwyck, sir? A gentleman left this for you." The security guard held an envelope with Brett's name on it.

Puzzled, Brett opened it. *Who left him a message?* The other members of the band crowded around as Brett silently read the message while they read over his shoulder.

Dear Brett, Eddie, Harry, and Peter;

It is with deep regret that I write this letter to inform you that you are broke.

Due to circumstances beyond my control, the money earned by the band Pink Melon has been lost in unstable investments.

I resign as your manager. You are now the property of Forthright Records and Management.

Sincerely,

Alistair "Lucky" Locke

P.S. Congratulations on winning the Grammy Award. I hope it is the first of many.

P.P.S. I will be leaving the country immediately and will not be available for communication.

P.P.P.S. If anyone with a scar running down the side of his face comes looking for me, be sure to tell him I'm not in the country anymore.

PLANS CHANGE

(BRETT RHYS-FALWYCK SOLO ALBUM: OCEANS)

Written and sung by Brett Rhys-Falwyck

I had it all figured out
you and me forever
a little house in the suburbs
a baby or two

Life would be perfect
walks in the park
ice cream with sprinkles
umbrella kisses in the rain

A dog, a cat,
laughter in the dark
warm cocoa in winter
snow angels on the lawn

Growing old together
hands always near
but I forgot to remember one thing
I never asked you

Plans change
Castaway dreams
adrift on ocean waves
like a message in a bottle

CHAPTER 6

*L*ucky's letter threw them all for a loop. No one expected to be broke just as their band was making it big. They didn't win any other awards that night, but the success they expected after the Grammy win didn't materialize like the members of Pink Melon expected.

Instead of adoring fans, they found creditors knocking at their doors with letters and liens and threats of lawsuits and worse. Brett didn't know what to do. They were advised to get a private investigator on the trail of the missing manager.

The four met at the pristine, glass-enclosed conference room of their management company and were told to sign a dissolution agreement or face charges of fraud and other felonious charges for the crimes Locke had perpetrated against the company in the band's name.

"Sorry, Brett, Harry, Eddie, Peter. We don't have any other option. We're dropping you. There's a clause in your contract that allows us to do this if we feel you acted in a morally or financially detrimental way." The executive who handed them the paperwork did look regretful, but it didn't make it any less painful.

"No hard feelings," Bryan said, handing them each a pen and pushing the dissolution agreement across the polished mahogany table.

"We have no options?" Cooly asked. He looked pale and scared. They all did.

Brett picked up the pen and signed his name with a flourish without even reading the contract. There wasn't anything they could do about this anyway. They didn't have the money to fight it, or take the management company to court, even though Brett was certain the company was just as guilty as Locke was for not catching the mismanagement of the band's funds.

"What does this mean?" Sticks asked as he signed his name.

"We're out. A one-hit wonder," Brett said, when no one else had the courage to speak up.

"Yeah, about that song . . ." Bryan Winston, slick in his dark suit and white shirt with his power red tie just perfectly knotted, licked his lips and leaned slightly away. Glancing toward the glass into the office area, where two other executives were nervously avoiding their gazes, Bryan cleared his throat.

"What about the song?" Brett said. His tone was cold, and a tight knot was forming in his stomach. He had a strong premonition this wasn't going to be good.

"That song was part of the band's inventory, and well, it doesn't belong to you anymore. It's part of the payment for the debt you owe us."

"What?" shouted Brett, vaulting to his feet. "What are you talking about? I wrote it. I put it together, I sound mixed it, I—"

"In our studios, at our expense, and in the original contract you signed, you all agreed to keep the band's inventory of songs with us for a span of five years or longer if we needed it to pay off debts incurred in organizing and arranging your appearances and so on." Bryan had flinched when Brett stood up so abruptly.

Out of the corner of his eye, he could see the security guard, a kindly old man with a face like Santa, hurrying toward them. The old man carried a pistol, but Brett wasn't even sure it was real. Usually the old man was quite nice, and he and Brett would often discuss the Super Bowl or other sports events. The old guy had a grandson Brett had signed a poster for just last week.

Sitting back down, head in his hands, Brett whispered, "Take it. Take it all. It doesn't matter anymore anyway."

"Brett," said Cooly softly, "we can fight this."

"How? How do we fight this?" Hands splayed on the table to keep from raising them into fists, Brett tried to keep the anger and frustration out of his voice. "Do you have a million lying around that I don't know about? We got nothing. Lucky took it all."

Bryan grabbed the paperwork and stood up abruptly. "Okay, gentlemen, that's all. I'll have Baxter show you out." He pointed to the door, careful to stay out of reach on the other side of the long table.

"Oh, and guys . . ." Bryan licked his lips again, the words he was about to say frozen on his lips as all four heads swiveled toward him, anger and defeat in all their eyes.

"What?" Brett finally said. "What else do you need? Want our souls, you motherfucking blood-sucking vampire?"

Bryan tittered at that, then straightened his shoulders. "No need to swear. I'm not the one who trusted all my money to a guy I barely knew. Lucky's actions have left you with nothing. We're dropping you. We keep the rights to your songs for the next ten years, of course. Even your cars, perks of the contract, were confiscated."

"Wait a minute," Harry bristled, stepping toward Bryan with anger in his eyes. "Those belong to us. They were gifts to us. Bonuses. I remember you clearly saying that when you gave us the keys."

"No, you misunderstood," said Bryan with a smug smile. "They were a loan, and we have taken them back. Your stuff has been removed from the cars and is waiting for you out in the anteroom. You can take everything when you go, or we will be happy to dispose of it for you."

"Bryan," said Brett coldly, rounding on the executive they'd all shared steaks and champagne with just weeks ago, "may you rot in fucking hell."

The four walked out to the elevator.

"Brett? Brett, wait a minute, I need a word with you."

Brett turned to see Bryan standing in the doorway they'd just walked through. He pointed to the table and chair Brett had just walked away from.

"What now? Need more blood?"

"No, no, nothing like that. I have something to discuss with you. Something I think you might want to hear."

"Brett?" said Cooly. The guys were standing by the elevator, waiting for him.

Brett hesitated, torn between leaving with his bandmates and curiosity about what Bryan wanted.

"Wait for me downstairs? I'll be right there," Brett said to Cooly.

Cooly nodded before turning to the other two. "Come on, boys, we need to figure out how we're getting out of here. Anyone got a credit card with them? Maybe we can Uber it?"

Brett watched the doors slide closed, the faces of his bandmates as shell-shocked as his own must look.

Seated once more at the table, Brett raised an eyebrow as he waited for Bryan to pull together some paperwork and approach him. The man leaned over Brett, the smell of his cologne so sickly sweet, Brett nearly gagged.

"We realize what happened was not entirely the band's fault. We are heartsick over it all, but business is business, and frankly, with the economy the way it is, we just cannot take on any more debt. Putting a band on the road is an expensive proposition, and with the win, we know your fans will expect a tour, and we just can't support it right now. Pink Melon's bank accounts were wiped out, and that means we still have debts to cover for bills already invoiced. I didn't tell everyone the worst of what is to come—you know the debt collectors will start calling soon."

Brett looked at Bryan in astonishment. "You mean you expect us to pay those debts out of pocket? Where do you think we're going to get that kind of money? I thought covering those debts was what you took our songs for?"

"That will cover part of it," Bryan agreed. He stopped pacing and gestured to someone outside the glass.

Brett turned as a woman in her early thirties entered. The pretty redhead was wearing a dark navy suit, white blouse, and sensible pumps. She carried a stack of papers in her arms. She was followed inside by two other equally stiffly dressed men in dark suits, white shirts, and loafers. They set more paperwork on the desk in front of him.

"Hello," said the woman, her voice soft and reassuring. Brett did a double take. This was the woman he'd slept with the time he had the shower dream. What was she doing here? He could see kindness and a little pity in her eyes. He narrowed his eyes but before he could speak, she nodded to the paperwork.

If she remembered him, she was great at hiding it. She didn't betray a single clue that they knew each other intimately. Of course, it had only been one time, and they'd both been a bit wasted, but surely he was memorable enough in bed for her to at least wink at him. Fine, two could play at that game. He kept quiet as well.

"My name is Amanda Harrison. This is Joe Barnes and Mark Thomas. We're part of the accounting team here."

"Amanda, Joe, and Mark are part of what we call our 'dream team' here," Bryan said. "They are very good at following the money."

"Following the money?" Brett was confused. First they told

them the money was gone, and now they were saying there might be some left. At least, that's what he assumed if they were following it.

"Bryan, why don't you let us explain what we do?" Amanda's voice was still soft, but firmer this time. She gestured toward the door. "Can you get us all some coffee?"

"I can't stay," Brett said, starting to stand up. "My friends are waiting for me downstairs."

"I think you'll want to hear this," Amanda said, fixing a steady gaze on him. All pity was gone from her eyes. Now there was only a firmness that spoke of confidence, and Brett found himself sitting back down before he realized it.

She pushed a packet of paperwork toward him and began explaining.

"So you think we can pay off the debt and find the rest of our money?" Brett asked a half hour later.

"That's what we hope. There are no guarantees. But it will take some time. So . . . Bryan thought that maybe you might want to help your friends and possibly sign on as a songwriter with the company for a period of no more than a year. With this steady flow of cash from your songs, which are quite good, by the way, we think we can stave off the hemorrhaging—the financial hemorrhaging that is—from the damage Mr. Locke created by his theft."

Brett stared at her, trying to process her suggestion. "If I sell my soul, you think my friends will be okay?"

"Don't think of it like that," Amanda said. She rubbed her eyes, and he realized with a start that she was trying to make the best of a bad situation. This was an out, a way to keep his friends and himself from filing for bankruptcy and losing their houses, at least.

"Think of it as a gift, a gesture of the love you have for those guys. And . . ." She stood, stretching her arms overhead and then, glancing his way, blushed a bit. Brett realized, with a start, she was trying to help him.

"Why?" he asked, pushing the books back to her.

"Why what?" she asked.

"Why help us? You don't even know us. What do you get out of this?"

"I get nothing out of this. It's the right thing to do." Amanda met his eyes without lowering her own.

He could see the dark ring around the blue widening as she stared at him. He felt like he was drowning in them.

"I will think about it," he said finally, standing up.

Without another word, he left the room and stepped into the waiting elevator. He was luckier than his bandmates. He'd bought his house himself. His car, a fancy Porsche, had never been one he liked anyway, but it suited the fans' expectations of his lifestyle, and he drove it for that reason. He wasn't sorry to see it go.

The elevator bumped as it stopped on a floor and opened to let in two guys in their late twenties. They punched the button for the basement as Brett listened with half an ear to their conversation.

"So, vacation time, dude. Where are you going?" one said to the other.

"Oh, this little ski resort area in Colorado near Telluride. It looks dope. Can't wait."

Brett's ears perked up at the words "Havenwood Falls," and he jerked his head around to look at them.

"I'm sorry to interrupt," he said apologetically, an urgency he didn't understand in his voice. "Did you say you're going to Havenwood Falls?"

The man's brows furrowed together. "Uh, no. Not even close. Never heard of the place."

The two exchanged a *what's with this guy* look until the one's eyes lit up with recognition of Brett's face. "Oh, dude, I know who you are! Sorry, man. Nah, I said Telluride. A ski town in Colorado. Here, I think I have a flyer about it somewhere."

The man patted his pockets and then handed Brett a flyer with snowcapped mountains, a skier, and a street filled with shops. It was like the one Brett had received in the mail the other day.

"Telluride," the guy said, pointing at the headline—right where the words *Havenwood Falls* were emblazoned in red lettering.

Brett looked at the guy to see if he was serious—which he seemed to be—then back at the words on the flyer. That now said "Telluride, Colorado."

Weird, Brett thought as he handed the flyer back to the man. *But what a strange coincidence.*

He stepped into the lobby, surprised to see his friends were still there waiting for him. He'd figured he'd been too long, and they would have left without him. His heart skipped a beat at their loyalty.

He took the bag with his stuff from Cooly and grinned. "Well, boys, it looks like we're back where we started."

"Yep, broke and disillusioned," quipped Harry as he grinned, the first real grin Brett had seen on his friend's face in a long time.

REFLECTIONS ON A POSSIBILITY

(BRETT RHYS-FALWYCK SOLO ALBUM: OCEANS)

Written and sung by Brett Rhys-Falwyck

I'm missing you in my bed
I'm whispering into the silence
just to hear my voice speak
I imagine you answering
smiles in the darkness
painting stars on the ceiling
An ocean of possibilities stretch before me
unclaimed and reflected in your eyes
The room grows dark too soon
Shadows fill the empty places
Memories of your promises
shake me aware
I want the silence back
the silence that is filled with you

CHAPTER 7

Weeks went by, and Brett hadn't made a decision yet. He knew the boys would say to tell the record company to "shove it where the sun don't shine," but he couldn't close the door to the possibility that he held the means to keep his friends and himself from bankruptcy.

He could help them. He could help them all. Why, then, did he hesitate?

There were three calls on his voicemail just from today: one from Bryan and two from Amanda, demanding his answer. They were about to set the hounds loose, and Brett knew what that meant.

Something stayed his hand from signing this blood contract, though, and he couldn't say what it was.

He'd tried for the last three weeks to get his mind off the band's troubles, but all he'd managed to do was bury them in a bottle. Vodka, whiskey, he didn't care. He wasn't a drunk, but that was before. Before Locke and the Grammys and the disappointment and fear he'd seen in the eyes of his friends.

"Some leader of the band you turned out to be," he chided

himself as he twirled a glass filled with amber liquid on the arm of the deckchair he was sitting in. He stared out at the ocean spread out in front of him in an endless series of repetitive waves, their white caps waving to him in a silent plea for him to come out and play with them. Their siren song was strong, and it took all his willpower not to get up and just start walking.

He didn't like to swim. This house by the ocean had been a gift intended for his mother—it was her dream to retire and live near the ocean. But he'd even managed to fuck that up. His timing, never good, really sucked when it came right down to it. Her death was still on his mind, more so lately than ever before.

"Sorry, Mom, I'm a horrible son," he said as he swallowed the contents of the glass in one swig.

Closing his eyes, he leaned back in the chair, the glass forgotten in his hands as he found himself drifting off to sleep, lulled by the lullaby of the ocean.

The grass under his bare feet was crisp and a brilliant shade of green. In his hand he held a parchment, a piece of yellowed paper older than he was. He wasn't sure how he knew this, but he knew it was true. He looked down in surprise to see he was wearing a long white gown, not unlike those nightgowns of old, something he would expect to see on Ebenezer Scrooge or someone from that time period. He floated, not quite touching the grass anymore as he neared the familiar boulder.

Sitting down, his back against the warm rock, he drifted to sleep.

His eyes snapped open at the sound of soft footfalls nearby. Glancing around the granite, he was, and yet wasn't, surprised to see the woman in white. Her blond hair flowed freely down her back, a golden river he wanted to swim in.

He stood.

He walked toward her. She stood with her back to him. She hadn't turned around yet. As he watched, her body shivered, her shoulders undulating as they gave birth to her wings. Brilliant white, they nearly blinded him.

He gasped.

The sound caused her to turn, her face hidden behind the silvery light that followed her form like a writhing snake, encompassing her in a gentle hug. He could see her mouth, soft and pink, open into a beautiful smile.

Her hands reached for him.

"Hello, lover," she whispered.

Her voice was unbelievably sweet, innocent and pure like a baby's. It soothed him.

"Come to Havenwood Falls. I'll be waiting," she said.

He felt his shoulders itching. Flexing his shoulder blades, he was shocked when a pressure, starting at the point of his shoulder blades, broke free of his skin to reveal his own wings in a pale, dove-gray color. They were so beautiful, he nearly cried. He twisted until he could hold the tip of one in his hand. The feathers were like a breath of air, floating and ethereal. They filled him with a peace he'd never known.

He smiled. He looked up. She watched him, her eyes a color like none he'd ever seen before. In their depths he saw pain, and forgiveness, and love. His hand reached for hers. He knew if he could touch her, he would be at peace. Nothing would ever hurt him again.

He woke as his shoulders were roughly shaken.

"Hey, Brett. Brett, are you okay? Come on, man. Stop this."

Brett slowly opened his eyes, angry he was being awoken and wanting to throttle whoever had taken him out of his dream place. Clouded eyes clearing, he saw Cooly standing beside him with a worried expression on his face.

Brett looked down and found his bare feet were rooted in sand, and the ocean was rinsing them as it ebbed and flowed around him. He felt the grittiness and grimaced, wishing he was on that soft grass again.

"You okay?" Cooly repeated, his tone worried.

Panic was reflected in Cooly's eyes as he looked at his friend.

Brett nodded slowly, his brain still fogged by alcohol and the dream. He wasn't sure what was real right at that moment.

"I'm fine," he said, grabbing Cooly for support as he found himself suddenly weak in the knees. What was he doing by the ocean? He looked behind him and saw he'd walked a good hundred yards without even being aware of leaving the deck.

"Let's go back inside. I have something to talk to you about," Cooly said. He gripped Brett firmly by the arm and half dragged the rocker back to the house.

Once inside, Cooly handed a tall glass of water to Brett and said, "Drink this, buddy. You need to lay off the hard stuff for a while."

Brett nodded. He took a long swallow of the water, finding it strangely refreshing. The fog in his mind was clearing, and he looked at Cooly in confusion. He hadn't spoken to his friend in days. Did he drunk-dial him? Did Cooly show up in time to keep him from taking that walk into the ocean because he called him?

"Why are you here?" Brett asked.

"The guys and I were worried. No one's heard from you in days. What have you been doing . . . besides drinking, and nearly taking a walk into the ocean, that is? Where did you think you were going to go? You do remember you don't know how to swim, right?"

Brett, looking sheepish, mumbled, "Wasn't going to swim, was going to fly."

"Yeah, and just exactly when did you sprout wings?"

Brett flexed his shoulders, the heavy weight of the wings gone from his back, and sighed. It was just a dream. Just another one of those crazy, stupid dreams.

"You have anything you want to tell me, dude?" said Cooly.

Brett caught an undertone of anger in Cooly's voice and wondered what that was all about.

"Not really sure where you're going with this tone." Brett studied Cooly, gauging his friend's face for clues to what was upsetting him. His eyes fell on the nearly empty bottle of whiskey on the table, and he licked his lips, wishing he could reach out for it for just one more taste. But he had a feeling Cooly wouldn't appreciate him being any more drunk than he already was.

"Did you know," Brett said with a lopsided grin, "you are fucking cute? I need to put the two of you together, though. It's hurting my eyes to look at you both. When'd you become a twin, anyway?"

Brett clapped his hands together, the images of Cooly staying doubled no matter how hard he tried to combine them into one.

Cooly watched him, his anger visibly increasing. He didn't speak. Instead, lips tightening to a thin line, he pulled a paper out of his pocket. It was one of those trade papers that catered to actors looking for auditions and other entertainment news. The article he thrust in Brett's face was a small one, just a few lines, written inside a box that outlined the short, three sentence announcement.

Brett closed his eyes, hoping when he opened them that the words would have stopped bouncing around. After a minute of concentrated effort, he was able to make sense of the article that had brought Cooly to his house in such a tizzy.

Singer-songwriter Brett Rhys-Falwyck, formerly of the band Pink Melon, and best known for his hit song "Love is Like a Memory," has signed a three-year contract with Forthright Records and Management Company. Mr. Rhys-Falwyck will be writing for the management company that formerly managed his band, Pink Melon, in a development capacity, and will report directly to the president of the company, Greg Granite.

Brett stared at the short article in shock. When had he agreed to this? He couldn't remember doing it. But here it was, in black and white, confirmation of his selling his soul to the company that had caused so much heartache to them all. Surely he wouldn't have done that. That would be like stabbing his friends and former bandmates in the heart. No wonder Cooly was so pissed. He would be, too, if one of the other guys had done that.

He racked his brain. Wait . . . That chick Amanda had come to his house . . . last week? The week before? Why couldn't he remember? He remembered she'd brought wine, and whiskey—good stuff too—and they'd grilled steaks. They'd had sex—that much he remembered.

He was so messed up right now. He needed a drink. No, he didn't need a drink.

Yes, he fucking did.

Getting up, he walked over to the wet bar and rummaged through the bottles under the bar until he found a semi-clean glass and the bottle of amber liquid he'd been eyeing since coming into the room.

Cooly, taking the bottle from him, said, "Brett, you've had enough of this. I need you to tell me what the hell this is all about. Is there any truth to this? I gotta tell you, the guys are fucking pissed. Really fucking pissed. Like they wanted to come over here and beat the shit out of you."

Brett took a long swallow of the liquid. Letting it burn down his throat, he squeezed his eyes shut tight, tears forming at the strong taste of the whiskey. He was tired all of a sudden—tired of being told what to do by people who didn't even know him and hadn't walked in his shoes. He deserved some respect. He deserved some credit for trying to keep them all solvent, if this article was true. Hell, he deserved . . . another drink. He reached for another bottle, not even caring what it was. Cooly snorted, but didn't stop him from drinking it. He could feel his friend's disgust as a tangible presence in the room, but he ignored it for the oblivion the alcohol promised.

His eyes fell on the flyer for Havenwood Falls, and he wished, not for the first time, that he could be there right now.

Cooly stood up. Striding over to his best friend, Cooly grabbed

Brett by the shoulders. Twisting him around, he said, "I can't help you anymore, man. I have problems of my own I need to take care of. You're on your own. If you really did this, if you really signed a contract with those . . . those—what did you call them?—'fucking blood-sucking vampires,' then you're on your own."

Brett, shaken by the tone of finality in his friend's voice, opened his mouth to argue, to defend himself. How could he explain to Cooly, or the other guys, that he'd sold his soul to the devil to save them all?

They wouldn't believe him. Hell, he didn't believe it. He didn't remember signing that contract. How had that happened? He couldn't have been that drunk, could he?

He opened his mouth to speak once more. When he turned around to face Cooly, the words froze on his lips as he saw the door close behind his best friend.

Possibly for the last time.

DRAWINGS IN THE SAND

(BRETT RHYS-FALWYCK SOLO ALBUM: OCEANS)

Written and sung by Brett Rhys-Falwyck

I am drawn to you like the tide to the shore
I have no choice
I have no voice
Being with you is an undeniable force

You pull me under
with the power of your love
I have no will, only float
staring at the stars above

I cannot stop the need for your touch
I have no will
I have no thrill
You are intoxicating, a drug I want too much

You pull me under
with the power of your love
I have no will, only float
staring at the stars above

Take me to heaven and throw me to Earth
I have no control
I have no soul
You have owned me since before my birth

You pull me under
with the power of your love
I have no will, only float
staring at the stars above

Like drawings in the sand
you leave me blank
Pull me under
Hold me forever

CHAPTER 8

ece frowned, the lines between her brows deepening the more she tried to solve the problem facing her on the computer.

"Can I help?"

Cecilia looked up to see Meghan standing in front of her with a raised eyebrow and a small smile.

"I hope so," Cece said with a frustrated laugh. She turned the computer screen so Meghan could see it. "I want to put up another flyer about the music camp. But every time I try to change this, it goes blank on me."

Meghan looked at the screen for a second and then grinned.

"Here. Just do this." She struck a couple of keys, and the image Cece was trying to create was suddenly there.

"Amazing," Cece said with a laugh. "I am headed out to get a coffee. Can I get you one for a change?" Cece asked the teen. "I owe you that, and so much more, for your help."

Meghan shook her head. "I'm fine," she said in a tone that implied she was not fine at all.

"Want to talk about it?" Cece asked as she gathered her purse and coat from behind the counter. She kept her tone casual, knowing how the girl valued her privacy.

"No, everything's fine," Meghan said. She met Cece's disbelieving expression with a bland one of her own.

Cece reached across the counter and squeezed the girl's wrist, careful not to allow any visions in. "You can trust me. You know that, right?"

Meghan nodded, lowering her eyes and turning when she heard Glenn's voice.

"Hey, Glenn," Cece said as she rounded the counter, "I need to run and get some coffee. Do you want anything?"

"Nope, I'm good," Glenn said. He squeezed Meghan's arm. "You okay?" he whispered to the girl.

She nodded.

"Watch the counter, then. I'll be back in a minute." Cece was out the door and down the street in a flash.

She had felt her wings twitching all day long and needed to be out in the cool air to still her warming blood. She needed to fly, but since her last foray out, when she'd once again run into her dream lover, she hadn't wanted to take the chance of encountering him.

That last dream had been too strange for her. He'd grown wings in her dream, beautiful dove-gray wings, and she'd had a strange urge to pull him with her into the sky. When he'd abruptly left the vision, she'd not only been surprised, but disappointed in his desertion of her.

"What'll you have?" Paisley, one of the local teens who worked as a part-time barista at Coffee Haven, asked with a pretty smile. Coffee Haven was busy as always.

"The usual," Cece said with a laugh.

Her order placed, Cece wandered around the shop a few minutes while she waited for her drink to be prepared. On one of the tables, she saw a paper. Picking it up, she realized it was one of those papers that listed events in the entertainment industry. She figured one of the tourists who had discovered Coffee Haven must have left it, because she didn't know of any place in town that would sell this kind of newspaper.

Her eyes were caught by the article about her rock star. "Hmmm . . . I wonder . . ."

Cece was lost in thought until Paisley called her name. Thanking her for the drink, Cece folded the newspaper and left the shop. Heading back to the music store, she decided to give it one more try.

"Here goes nothing," she thought as she typed out her request to the Forthright Records and Management Company and addressed the email to Brett Rhys-Falwyck.

BRETT WALKED into the glass-enclosed conference room to find he was facing not just Amanda, but her whole team *and* the president of the company. They were all dressed in dark suits and wore even sterner expressions. Spread out before them were the contracts he had supposedly signed that day Amanda had visited him.

He was alone. He hadn't told Cooly or any of the others what he was planning to do. To be honest, he didn't really know what he was planning to do. He hadn't hired a lawyer, hoping they could settle this on their own without involving expensive attorneys and courts. He thought he was sparing them all, both the band and the management company, the embarrassment of false accusations and recriminations by doing this between friends instead of as adversarial opponents. He'd hoped they would meet him on similar grounds, but they obviously wanted to bring in the big guns.

Greg Granite looked him in the eye and didn't smile as he offered his hand. Brett shook it, not surprised to find the man's hand smooth and slippery. Everything about the slick company president said he was not to be trusted. Sunday school admonitions from their minister about watching out for the one with the forked tongue rose to his mind. He met the man's eyes, not surprised to find no sympathy in the dark irises. Somehow that set the tone for the whole meeting.

Brett looked at Amanda. Her new position obviously came with a bigger paycheck, as she was now sporting some pretty expensive jewelry. She didn't meet his eyes. Her smile seemed tight, and he noticed fine lines radiating from her bright red painted lips. Why hadn't he noticed this hard edge about her before? Because he wasn't paying attention. He'd lost his reason for living, for trying. He realized suddenly that he hadn't noticed she wasn't the kind of woman he should have been with because he didn't care anymore.

She was the kind of woman his mother called a chameleon. She would change herself to match her surroundings, her survival depending on her ability to blend in and be just like everyone else.

Brett felt all the anger leaving him as he looked at her through his new revelations. She wasn't evil. She was just immature. A child. Her wants and needs took precedence over what was decent and right. She was no better or worse than a spoiled teenager.

He slid his glance from her to the rest of the people in the room. None of them would meet his eyes. They knew. They knew what she'd done and didn't care. All that mattered to them was the bottom line, and he was just one more signature among the hundreds of signatures they had on paperwork they collected like a devil collected souls. They owned him.

He realized then that he wasn't going to get them to right the situation just by asking for it. The decent thing didn't exist in this room. There was nothing he could say or do that would make them stop this merry-go-round and let him off.

He would have to make a decision about how much he wanted to air his dirty laundry in public to get them to tear up this fraudulent contract. They were counting on him being too embarrassed to admit he'd been drunk, or on drugs, or whatever she'd done to him to get him to sign that paper, making him a slave to their bottom line.

He could do it. He could take them all down—maybe not the president, but at least Amanda and the two suits who were always with her—but he wasn't sure what he would gain by it. It wasn't just him he would be destroying. It would also be the band. And Pink Melon was more than just him, it was all of them. This was not a decision he could make without the others' permission. They would be dragged into it, too.

He hesitated to sit as indicated while he considered the ramifications of his decision if he chose to go forward. Weighing the pros and cons, he could see the smug smile on the president's face, the fear in Amanda's eyes, and the bored, unconcerned look on the faces of her two henchmen. He could bring the company down, but he would also damage the reputation of a band he loved and the people, he realized, he loved just as much.

Did Cooly deserve that? Or Harry? Or Peter? Or any of their families? How far did he need to take this?

All this went through his mind in the seconds it took him to sit and study his opponents.

He stood. Decision made.

Without a word, he walked from the room toward the elevator. Before the doors closed behind him, he thought he saw respect in the eyes of Amanda. And regret.

But he wasn't going to live his life with regrets anymore.

He was just going to live his life.

MESSAGE

(BRETT RHYS-FALWYCK SOLO ALBUM: OCEANS)

Written and sung by Brett Rhys-Falwyck

I saw a white owl the other day
swooping gracefully on
wings spread wide as it floated on thermals
and I thought of you

A lonesome call
echoed across the snow
mirroring my own as
I cried out for you

Overhead an ocean of gray
sandwiched the white sand
I walked to the edge of forever
wishing for you

and I found a bottle with a message inside
Uncurling the paper, I saw a single heart
I smiled, knowing you'd smile too, as the wind
took the message to you

CHAPTER 9

Ding! Brett heard the sound of the alert on the computer in the other room as it signaled a message had just come in. He stiffened, trying to ignore it. How had that message gotten through? He was sure he'd turned his computer off, loathing the hate he saw in the messages from fans who thought he'd sold out his friends when the news broke of his deal and the demise of Pink Melon. If they only knew their hatred of him was nothing compared to his own feelings of disgust.

The machine dinged again. He must have turned it on without realizing it.

Setting his coffee down on the kitchen counter, he sighed. Why avoid the inevitable? It was probably from the lawyer, needing his signature on a document or wanting to share news about the fraud case against the management company that he'd filed last week.

So far, things had not gone well. They'd filed a countersuit claiming he was in violation of the very agreement he was arguing he hadn't signed. The case was destined to be tied up in court for years, with accusations flying back and forth faster than the Concorde, but meanwhile, he was unable to do anything until it was settled. Brett was prepared to wage the battle for as long as necessary, but didn't want to drag it out so long that it became pointless or that he became broke.

When he reached the computer, he was surprised to see the email was from the management company.

"Well, well, maybe they are ready to do the right thing," Brett mumbled as he opened the email.

But it wasn't about the lawsuit. It was from a secretary he'd never heard of before. "Brad Longstreet," he read the name out loud, rolling the name on his tongue.

Dear Mr. Rhys-Falwyck:

This email came for you the other day from someone I assume is a fan, regarding a music camp for teens that is in the works at a small town in Colorado called Havenwood Falls. I wasn't sure what to do with it, and as both Amanda Harrison and Greg Granite are out of the office, I figured I would just forward it to you and let you decide what you want to do about it. I hope you don't mind. Attached is the information regarding the music camp. It sounds pretty cool.

Have a wonderful day and if you need anything, don't hesitate to ask.

Sincerely,

Brad Longstreet

Forthright Management Company

666 Diablo Street

Los Angeles, CA

THE CURSOR HOVERED over the attachment. Brett wasn't sure he wanted to know anything about this. A music camp? What was that all about? And what were the odds it was in the exact same ski town on that flyer he'd received some time ago? He googled Havenwood Falls, but found no information.

He clicked the attachment anyway, curiosity piqued.

Reading quickly, he was surprised at the sender's detailed description of the camp and what its goals were, along with instructions on how to contact her (send back his agreement or declination of the invitation).

"Oh, what the hell," he muttered as he pressed the keys and sent off a response.

Going back to the kitchen for his now lukewarm coffee, he had barely taken a sip when his computer dinged again.

Cecelia, owner of a small music shop in town, had responded, wanting to know what he would charge, and he took a moment to consider his answer. Never having done this before, he was not sure what to charge.

Finally he sent a response and let her know he would do it for free if she would make a donation to his favorite charity—one that benefited disabled musicians—in an amount she deemed appropriate.

He sipped again, waiting for her response.

The ding was very quick, causing him to smile. She had attached three files. One had the name and phone number of a Melissa Richter, who rented cabins, with instructions he was to call her and have the charges for the cabin sent to Cecilia Amundson at Havenwood Falls Music & More. He clicked open the second attachment after writing down information from the first one.

The second file contained information about where to meet the bus that would take him to Havenwood Falls with a firm command, for its tone was nothing but a command, on where to leave his car, as he wouldn't need it in town.

The third attachment was a copy of the flyer announcing the camp and asking him to attach any corrections to the email and return with his approval, whether changes were to be made or not, within twenty-four hours.

He glanced over it quickly, and made a suggestion to limit the class to just six students to allow for a more one-on-one feel. He suggested also that the camp agenda be included so the students would know what they were going to learn. He added a few lines of suggestions for the agenda to include learning to write lyrics, add music to it, how to perform, and then asked if they could do a small concert featuring the students' songs on the last night of the camp.

He closed his email by suggesting they continue to correspond via email to confirm details. After hitting send, he waited to see what her response would be.

He was suddenly antsy as his computer remained silent. Eerily silent. He didn't realize just how quiet his world had become lately until the computer stopped dinging.

Taking his phone with him, he went out on the deck and seated himself. Ignoring the shakes that came on with a sudden chill breeze, he closed his eyes. He wanted a drink.

He needed a drink.

CECELIA CONTAINED HER EXCITEMENT, barely, when she got the email back. At first she thought it might be a prank, but no one was watching her, and she knew if Glenn had perpetuated this email as a joke, he'd be waiting for her reaction.

"Excuse me," said a male voice.

Cecelia looked up from the computer screen and stopped typing. In front of her was the young man she'd seen Meghan talking to once or twice when Glenn wasn't around. He had an aura of danger and malevolence around him. Narrowing her eyes, she studied him. Dark hair, dark eyes, pale skin. He didn't have a feeling of magic around him, and his bearing wasn't arrogant, just petulant. She didn't sense evil, but there was a strangeness in his eyes that bothered her. Here was someone who could become evil, the kind of kid who might grow up to do terrible things. She reached for his hand, then pulled back when his eyes widened at her movement and he flinched back slightly, moving just out of reach.

Why don't you want me to touch you? she wondered. Something about him felt like a contained explosion, although she couldn't really explain why.

"May I help you?' She smiled, the smile not quite reaching her eyes, but not unfriendly.

"I'm supposed to meet someone here," he said. He pointed to the list for the recording studio that sat on the counter next to the cash register. "I'm due to go into the recording studio. Do I need a key?"

Cecelia nodded, handing him a key on a large wooden dowel, purposely attached to it with a chain so that no one would accidentally take the key.

"Whom are you meeting? I only see your name on the list . . ."

"There you are."

Cecelia looked up as Meghan joined the boy and took him by the arm.

"Come on," the girl continued. She tossed Cecelia a glance that begged her silence. "We don't have much time. Did you bring it?"

"Yeah," the boy said with an annoyed expression. "I'm not sure about this . . ."

Meghan bent her head closer to the boy's and whispered something in his ear that made him relax and grin. When he smiled like this, his aura changed. Cecelia felt an uncomfortable feeling in the pit of her stomach. With a sudden realization that shocked her, she got a strong feeling of love and possessiveness emanating from the boy.

Cecelia wondered if Meghan knew that he liked her, not just

liked her, but *really* liked her. Cecelia closed her eyes for a moment, and when she opened them again, she saw Meghan pulling the boy to the back of the store and enter the recording studio. The lights went on in the room. The boy set his gig bag against the chair and pulled his guitar from it. As she watched the two of them fiddling with dials and him tuning his guitar, she looked around for Glenn, before remembering he'd left to go to a dentist appointment and wouldn't be back for another hour at least.

In a minute, Meghan was at the microphone and the boy was playing the guitar. He couldn't take his eyes off Meghan, but she was all about whatever she was singing. Periodically she stopped, fiddling with dials again and starting over. She was smiling from ear to ear, and the boy with the guitar was, too. Cecelia was sure his smile had nothing to do with the song, but rather the singer.

"What's that all about?" she muttered before turning her attention to a customer.

The store was busy enough that for the next hour Cecelia forgot about Meghan and the boy in the recording studio. She sent the information to Brett, responding to his questions with answers as best she could. She asked him, with her final email, to confirm when he'd made his arrangements to come so that she could put in place his other arrangements to get him to town.

Printing off the flyers now that his participation was confirmed, she set a few on the counter and put one up on the entrance door so people would see it when they came into the store, and one on the other side so they'd see it when they left. She took his advice and made the camp small, limiting it to six, as it was her first event.

She called the Havenwood Falls Arts Council and asked if she could use the Annex for a final concert where each student would showcase their original songs. Since the event was for charity, the Council was thrilled to allow access. The Annex was an old warehouse south of town square that had been transformed into an industrial-chic multipurpose building. It included an art gallery, space for a market, and a theater used for both live and cinematic performances. Its acoustics were perfect for their mini-concert.

Heart thumping with joy, Cecelia greeted customers and made her way to the back of the store. As she reached the recording studio, Meghan and the boy emerged. Meghan was skipping slightly, holding the boy's elbow as they made their way to the front of the store.

Meghan was so excited, she didn't notice the door opening. Glenn entered just as Meghan hugged the boy with the guitar. Cecelia, still in the back of the store, watched as Glenn stopped, face pale, as he noticed Meghan hugging the other boy.

The other boy hugged her back, a little tighter than necessary.

"Meghan?" Glenn said in a small, tight voice. He looked gray. His eyes looked hurt and confused.

Cecelia hurried toward the front of the store as Meghan turned and tried to get out of the boy's embrace. The boy moved slightly in front of Meghan as she moved toward Glenn, blocking her passage.

He'd set his guitar down and looked ready to do battle. He looked more than ready; he looked like he'd like nothing better than to fight Glenn. Judging by the way Glenn's hands were balled into fists, he was ready for it, too.

Meghan slipped around the boy and smiled at Glenn. "Hey, Glenn . . . ummm, this is Laine Greenhill. He's . . ."

"I know who he is." Glenn's tone was flat and angry. He stared at Laine as if he could will the other boy to leave. Glenn crossed his arms and puffed out his chest in a parody of a male mating ritual, and Cece wasn't sure what to do. Right now, the two boys were pretty civil, but if things looked to be going down the other path, she would step in.

Cece had learned long ago not to get in the middle of a turf war, and this was shaping up into that very thing. She hadn't smelled magic or supernatural capabilities on Laine, and she knew Glenn was a human, so she figured the worst she might expect were a few fists flying, but both boys just continued to stare at each other as if waiting for the other to move first. Meghan fluttered between the two, not quite sure whom to placate first.

Finally, Laine stepped forward with his hand extended and said, "Nice to meet you."

His eyes were as flat and cold as Glenn's. It was obvious neither boy was happy to see the other, but neither wanted to be the first to show it in front of Meghan. They were still just sizing each other up.

To give her credit, Meghan didn't give anyone preference, keeping her distance from both when it became apparent they weren't going to fight.

Cecelia, deciding bloodshed in her store wasn't the best way to get more customers, stepped between them and said, "Hey, Glenn, glad you're back. I need your help at the front."

She didn't give him a chance to object. Taking him firmly by the elbow, she steered him behind the counter where the flyers rested.

Meghan left with the boy, tossing an apologetic glance Glenn's way, which he purposely ignored. The hurt look on her face at Glenn's rejection broke Cece's heart.

"What do you need me to do?" he asked.

Cecelia heard the defeat in his voice and squeezed his arm in sympathy. He shrugged her hand away.

"I heard from him," Cecelia said as a distraction. She pointed to the computer and the email she had pulled up.

Glenn jerked his head toward her, his jaw open in shock.

"You mean you heard from that Pink Melon guy?" He sounded like he didn't believe her.

Cecelia nodded and couldn't keep from grinning. "He agreed to do it. And he's doing it for free. Just asked me to make a donation to a foundation that helps disabled musicians."

"Wow! Oh, wow! So when is it going to be?"

Cecelia pointed to the flyer, and he read the dates. Brow wrinkling as he thought, he said, "Why so few participants?"

"A couple of reasons. First, it is the first one I am doing, and I want it to be awesome. Second, he wants to be able to work closely with everyone. Third, since we are doing some of it here in the recording studio, and some of it at the Annex, we wanted to make sure everyone got equal time and attention and that we can coordinate it well. The logistics of getting between here and the Annex would be harder with more students. And, I already have interest from a few kids—someone named Zoey, Elliot Martin, William Kasun, and I'm hoping you and Meghan will want to attend, too. "

"Meghan? Why Meghan? She can't play an instrument."

"Have you heard her sing? She's got an amazing voice. If nothing else, she can sing all your songs."

"Yeah, she does have a great voice." While his words were praising, his eyes darkened with renewed hurt from Meghan leaving with another boy.

Cecelia scrambled to keep him distracted. "Um . . . I know it's during your birthday, Glenn, but I hope you'll come?"

"Sure. Wouldn't miss it. I can help with some of the stuff in the recording studio. And I can help drive people around."

"Great," said Cece with a grateful squeeze on his arm. "Now, we just need to finalize some of the details."

Glenn nodded. He looked at the flyer listing the time and date of the concert and said, "I'll go hang these at a couple businesses, if that is okay with you? Places the kids all go. I would put one up at school, but they don't let us hang stuff up. But I can announce it on the morning announcements. I can hand some of these out to people I know who might be interested in coming to the show afterward."

"That would be great," Cecelia said, relieved that he had

volunteered to help her get the word out. "And Glenn, I am so glad you want to come."

"Wouldn't miss it. It'll give Meghan and me a chance to do something without Romeo—Laine—interfering."

Glenn left with the flyers to hang some around town.

Cece looked down at the sign-up sheet she had on the counter and saw one more name had been added on the list.

Uh-oh, she thought when she saw the last name, *this might be trouble.*

Laine Greenhill was written below Meghan's name.

THE SANDS OF TIME

(BRETT RHYS-FALWYCK SOLO ALBUM: OCEANS)

Written and sung by Brett Rhys-Falwyck

Lazy Sunday morning
rain on the windowpane
and I let myself go
I let myself go
Whispered conversations
told in the rustlings of sheets
secrets unfold
secrets unfold
Time passes like sand
in the hourglass
silence breaks
silence breaks
Sighs fall like leaves
before winter snow
waiting
waiting

CHAPTER 10

*N*ot for the first time, Brett wondered what he was thinking, then he wondered if he had time for a drink. Reluctantly, he turned from the airport bar with its tantalizing cornucopia of liquor on shelves set against the back wall to the bottle of plain water he set on the table in front of him.

Things were progressing with the lawsuits, and he'd told his lawyer he was going out of town for a few days to work on a music camp with some high school kids, something the lawyer said would be great publicity and make him look good in the eyes of the court, so he approved the trip. Not that he needed his lawyer's approval to know he was doing the right thing, but it still made him feel a little better that at least there was some action going on. Doing *something* was better than doing *nothing*, as his mother used to say.

Fueled by the memory of his mother, he'd left his house with little trepidation, but now that he was actually here, he was having second thoughts. And third thoughts. And fourth thoughts.

Brett wished his lawyer had stopped him from going. What if he hated it there? It was Colorado, after all. And it was April. How crazy did a California guy have to be to go to a state like Colorado during a time when the weather could be so unpredictable?

"Pretty darn crazy," he muttered as he took a long swallow of the cool water. It soothed his throat, and he found he didn't even miss the harder stuff he'd gotten into the bad habit of drinking lately. His mother would be proud of him.

He smiled, a slow grin that spread across his face, lightening his mood considerably. A woman, dressed for business in a dark pantsuit and white blouse, looked over at him with a welcoming grin, thinking his smile was for her. He ignored her, turning instead to look at a harried mother with three children tugging at her clothing as she tried to pay for their fries and chicken tenders.

Her panicked expression as she looked through her bags for her wallet touched him, and he stood up, not realizing what he was doing until he got there. He took out his wallet, handed the guy behind the counter his card, and paid for her food.

"Oh, thank you," she said with a grateful expression. "I know my wallet is here someplace, but . . ." She spread her hands to her three children who were now standing close to her, eyes wide and curious, as if for protection from the stranger.

"Here you go," the guy said, handing Brett the tray and his card.

"Oh, here, I'll take that," the woman said. She was rooted to the spot by her children, all of whom continued to stare at him with those silent, wide-eyed stares that reminded him of the Precious Moments statues his mother used to collect.

"It's okay, I don't mind," he said with a gentle smile. He walked toward one of the larger tables with several chairs and set the tray of food down.

"Enjoy," he said as he walked back to his table, where he'd left his briefcase containing his laptop and some paperwork he needed to finish for the lawyer. Energized by his act of charity, Brett felt a lot more lighthearted than he had just moments before.

The woman who'd smiled at him got up as a flight was announced. He realized with a start that it was his flight, too. He followed the woman toward the gate. She slowed her steps until he caught up. He was so lost in thought, he barely heard her speak.

"That was very kind of you," she said with a flip of her hair as she stepped beside him. She matched her steps to his, and they arrived at the assigned gate at the same time.

He didn't answer. Her approval wasn't needed for his gesture of generosity, and he honestly didn't want to stand out. He nodded, handed the flight attendant at the entrance to the plane his ticket, and stepped inside the plane.

"You're Brett Rhys-Falwyck, aren't you?" said the woman.

He started, turned, and looked at her.

"No," he said, regret in his tone. "I wish I was."

He ignored her puzzled expression at his abrupt answer and took his assigned seat near the window. A few minutes later, a woman took the seat beside him. She was grandmotherly in appearance, with fluffy white hair and a large bag, which he helped her store in the overhead bin. She sat down and pulled out a book, promptly ignoring him.

Brett looked out the window, thoughts everywhere but where he was. The plane took off with relatively little effort, inertia pushing him back into his seat. In a few minutes, he was asleep, his dreams chaotic.

"Sir. Sir, would you like a drink?"

Brett jerked awake. Opening his eyes, he blinked a few times to bring himself back to the present.

"No, thank you," he mumbled to the attendant, who was waiting for an answer.

She moved on to the people in the rows behind him. He could hear the squeaking wheel of the cart fading as she moved farther down the aisle.

"You okay, dear?" the old woman asked. She set the book down in her lap, pulled her glasses down her nose, and turned slightly to look him in the face, reminding him immediately of Mrs. Simkins, his third-grade teacher. She'd been his favorite teacher, taking extra time with him whenever he needed help.

And then she shifted, her face changed, and for a second, he was sure he was looking at his mother's face. Same blue eyes, same trick with the glasses, and same way of looking at him like whatever he had to say was the most important thing she had to hear that day.

He was instantly at ease with this stranger, which was probably why he started talking and couldn't stop. Keeping his voice low, he told her about the dream, about the trouble his band was in, and about this strange offer to teach a music camp in a town he'd never heard of and couldn't find on any map.

"I'm not sure why I'm even going," he finally admitted. He rubbed his eyes, suddenly overwhelmed and tired, before continuing. "I'm not even sure *where* I'm going. For all I know, some crazy fan has set this whole thing up like something out of a Stephen King book. I wouldn't mind it so much, but not finding the town on a map is kind of worrisome to me."

"Oh, you will find your way, I'm sure," the woman said with a chuckle. She slipped her finger between the pages of her book to hold her place, and he silently applauded her for not dog-earing the page—he hated when people damaged books like that. She leaned in closer and whispered, "Havenwood Falls is a delightful town. You will like it very much. Are you a skier?"

Her expression hadn't changed from its former kindness, but he could see she wasn't thinking of him as a skier by the way her tone rose slightly.

"No," he said with a chuckle. "Not my thing. I'm going there just for the music camp I'm running."

"Oh, that will be nice, dearie," the woman said. She seemed reassured he wouldn't be skiing, and he was almost offended by her certainty he couldn't do it. "Well, be sure to stop by Coffee Haven and try their blueberry scones."

She gave him a wink, then leaned back into her seat and picked her book up again.

"Are you from Havenwood Falls?" he asked.

She glanced at him with a blank look in her eyes. "Never heard of it. I'm from Telluride."

And with that, she went back to her reading.

Behind them, Brett heard a group of people talking about skiing and their plans when they arrived at the airport in Telluride, where Brett was to meet his ride to Havenwood Falls. It appeared almost everyone on the plane was going to the same place. The fellow behind him stood up and reached over the seat to slap Brett on the shoulder.

Not too much later, the fasten seatbelt sign lit up, and the attendants began to prepare for descent as an announcement came over the loudspeaker.

"Hello, this is your captain, Brad, speaking. The temperature is a balmy twenty degrees in Havenwood Falls, the ski slopes have a nice new coating of powder, and I hear the beer and hot cocoa are flowing at the resort. Be sure to stop by Coffee Haven and have one of their specials for me. And a famous blueberry scone. Just remember to stop at just one, or you might need to buy new pants."

"The pilot must really like Havenwood Falls—and those scones," Brett said with a chuckle.

"Do you mean Telluride?" the old woman asked. "I didn't hear him talk about any place else."

Brett, certain he'd heard the pilot say Havenwood Falls, was beginning to think this woman had lost her mind. Kind of like the guy in the elevator back in LA. *Maybe it's me losing my mind*, Brett thought. Shaking his head, he took a deep breath, a sudden giddiness overcoming him. Something about this was setting all his nerves on fire, and he couldn't wait to get there.

"Havenwood Falls, here I come," he whispered. And he liked the sound of it.

Thoughts of the band, legal troubles, and missing his mother disappeared into the back of his thoughts as he settled into his seat for the landing.

~

"SIR? ARE YOU MR. FALWYCK?" a polite voice at his side drew Brett's attention from the luggage return. He was waiting for his suitcase to make its way around the carousel to where he stood with a very excited group of skiers and others. The woman in the business suit had been met by an equally professionally dressed man and left with him, tossing him a backward glance as if saying, "Sorry, you lost your chance," but little did she know, what she offered was old news to him, and he wasn't interested in flings anymore, no matter how nice the legs were.

"Rhys-Falwyck," he said out of habit. For some reason, people had a problem with the hyphenated name all the time. "Better yet, just call me Brett."

He turned, hand held out to shake the hand of the small black man standing before him with a clipboard. The man was smiling, his dark eyes warm and gentle as they met Brett's. He wore a name badge that proclaimed his name as "Brad."

"Are you ready? The bus is about to leave," Brad said as he checked off Brett's name. Brett noticed the list contained about twenty names and his was the last.

"Yep," Brett said as he grabbed his guitar case and suitcase, which had finally made their way around to him. "Lead the way."

When he felt the cold blast of air that felt more like winter than spring, he was glad he'd worn his thick leather coat and scarf. He shuffled his bags in both hands and strode quickly behind the man to the bus. Handing over his suitcase, he held on to his guitar, refusing to slide it into the luggage compartment under the bus.

"Okay, everyone," Brad said from the front of the bus once everyone was loaded. "Havenwood Falls welcomes you to what will probably be the last ski runs of the season. Be safe and have fun! The trip from Telluride is about an hour around the mountains, so sit back and enjoy the views."

A few whistles and comments were heard from the back of the bus, where a very enthusiastic group of skiers were seated. The noise level on the bus rose as they left the airport and headed toward their destination.

Brett watched the scenery pass by, mostly white and very pretty with tall mountains and quaint houses and farms dotting the landscape as they drove toward Havenwood Falls.

He saw a sign that proclaimed they were about six miles away when his eyes were caught by movement in the nearby woods that sandwiched the road on either side. He could have sworn it was a wolf, but by the time he scanned the forest for confirmation, the animal, if he'd ever even been there, was gone.

As they pulled onto the town's main street, Brett's breath caught in his throat. It was beautiful. A coating of white powder, snow still gently falling, covered all the buildings and sidewalks. The center of town was a large square space he assumed was green when not covered with snow. It contained a beautifully built gazebo, and the buildings that surrounded it were quaint and definitely intended to attract tourists.

He saw signs for Whisper Falls Inn, a bookshop, gift and jewelry stores, and an herbal shop. Coffee Haven looked popular, and he noted several people holding paper cups and small packages, in which he assumed were some of those famous blueberry scones. Everywhere he looked, most of the people were smiling and laughing. Skis leaned haphazardly against the sides of buildings like a windblown fence. Outside seating areas were occupied by people sipping hot beverages or wine in spite of the cold weather. Brightly colored coats worn by people walking around the area only added to the festive air of the town.

Brad stood up and clapped to get everyone's attention. "We're here. If you need help finding anything, let me know. The inn is directly behind the bus, the coffee shop is that direction as you leave the bus, and your luggage will be on the sidewalk in just a minute. Please do *not* reach into the luggage compartment on your own. I am happy to do that for you."

In a few minutes, every bit of luggage was unloaded and waiting to be claimed. Brett reached for his just as the older woman who'd sat next to him on the plane reached for hers.

"It was nice to meet you, dearie," the woman said. She waved to a woman and child who were waiting for her. "Do you know where you're going?"

"I think so." Brett pulled a paper from the inside pocket of his jacket. It had instructions on where he was to meet Cecelia, and then she would arrange transportation to the cabin he would rent while he was here.

He was to start the camp in two days. She wanted to give him time to get acclimated, and for that, he was grateful. Especially as he breathed in the crisp, cool air, and was reminded of the thinner air at this altitude. He'd certainly have to adjust his breathing before trying to sing.

There was something wonderfully refreshing about Havenwood Falls, and he was suddenly excited about the prospect of exploring it.

"Where do you need to go?" she asked as he walked with her toward her family.

"To Havenwood Falls Music & More," he said, reading from the paper.

"Oh yes, that's just over there. See it?" She pointed down the street. "Right across from the gazebo."

"Thanks," Brett said, seeing the shop's sign. Shouldering his guitar and grabbing his suitcase, he started walking in the direction she indicated. The smell of coffee was intoxicating as he passed several people holding the paper cups. He slowed, looking around the street in surprise. There was something about the town's atmosphere that was so heavy, it weighed on him like a wool coat, comfortable and familiar, and yet so strange, he shivered.

It felt like home. He mentally shook off the feeling. How could it feel like home? He'd never been here before.

In a few minutes, he found himself in front of the place he was looking for. On the front, a neon orange light announced the store was open for business. Through the windows, he could see stacks of records, CDs, and signs proclaiming different departments. He saw customers browsing through items in the store. On the back wall, a few guitars were hung, gleaming in the dull light. His hand closed over the strap to his gig bag, where his own guitar rested.

He saw a young boy, about seventeen with broad shoulders and a big smile, chatting with a pretty dark-haired girl. He saw a woman at the counter, her back to him as she rang up the purchase of a customer. Outside the store, a couple of high-school-aged girls hung around, watching the boy inside with hungry eyes.

He wanted to put this moment in a song. Grabbing his ever-present notebook, he took out the pen he had attached to the spiral binding and wrote a few sentences, humming a tune as he stood there.

Invisible man, he wrote, *standing on the corner of the rest of his life.* He paused, the pen poised over the page as he considered where to go next. *Not sure which way to turn. One way and his life will change, the other way and it will stay the same.*

"Hey mister," said a girl, giggling at her boldness as she touched him on the arm. "Can I have your autograph?"

He blinked, looking at her in surprise, curious as to how she knew who he was.

"The sign," the girl said with another giggle. She pointed to the door where a small picture of him was hung. It contained the information about the upcoming music camp.

"Sure," he said. Taking the proffered paper from her, he smiled as he signed it. "Do you want a picture, too?"

"Already got one," the girl said, holding up her phone as she leaned close to him as he signed the autograph for her.

Brett raised an eyebrow at the picture the girl had taken. It showed him looking wistfully into the store, and the second one was of him writing in his notebook.

"What did you write?" the girl asked as she took the autographed paper from him.

"Oh, just some snatches of lyrics," he answered, shoving the notebook back into his pocket.

Shouldering his guitar and luggage, he excused himself and watched the two girls run off down the street giggling. A small smile spread across his face. Some things never changed.

Stepping into the shop, he was first struck by the warmth that hit his face, in contrast to the cold snowy weather outside, and second by the comfortable, peaceful atmosphere of the store. The conversations were muted, like the buzzing of bees in a meadow.

The store smelled like dusty cardboard and an herbal scent he couldn't identify but probably had something to do with the candles burning in a few strategic places around the store. He also caught the subtle odor of wax, the kind used on guitar strings to keep them from drying out.

He immediately relaxed, not even realizing how tense he had been before he walked in.

"Hello, welcome to Havenwood Falls. I'm Cece, the one who contacted you. We're so glad you're here," said a soft voice at his elbow.

He smelled her perfume before he saw her. It reminded him of sun-drenched meadows. Soft, floral, and pleasant. Just like her, he realized when he turned to greet her and was struck dumb at her beauty. *Such a cliché reaction*, he thought, *but wow, she was beautiful.*

And she was the woman in his dreams.

DARK SIDE OF FOREVER

(BRETT RHYS-FALWYCK SOLO ALBUM: OCEANS)

Written and sung by Brett Rhys-Falwyck

There is no guarantee of a happily ever after
nothing says tears are followed by laughter
life doesn't come with a handbook you know
we do the best we can as we go

Nothing is for certain 'cept death and taxes they say
Me, I'll take the taxes and not give death sway
too much time spent on the dark side of forever
and I forget to never say never

If you cannot stay
then please go away
and leave me to my pain
never darken my door again

The dark side of forever lies.
It's a place without you
a place where dreams do
not exist and hope dies

CHAPTER 11

*T*he thought that this woman was *her* stopped the words at the back of Brett's throat. *It could not be possible, could it?* To hide his confusion, he put his guitar down and set the suitcase next to it at the counter, avoiding making a fool of himself by wrapping her in a hug. How could his dream woman be here of all places? He had to be imagining it. Things like this did not happen in real life, and yet, somehow, looking at her, the way his breath caught and his heart pounded, he knew it had to be true.

Cece, slender and blond, walked to the other side of the counter, where she helped a customer before turning the full effect of her smile on him.

His eyes were trapped by her mouth. Why was it so familiar? He found himself wanting to touch those full, soft pink lips, and had to shove his hands in his pockets to maintain his composure.

Her smile twisted slightly as if reading his mind, but otherwise she said nothing, waiting for him to speak.

Clearing his throat, he said, "So, what's next? Do you need me to hang out here and meet people, or will I need to find a ride to the cabin?"

"I will have Glenn take you to the cabin. Would you like to go now? You can drop your stuff off there and come back here with Glenn, or you can stay there for the rest of the day and come here tomorrow. The store is open this Sunday for a brief meet and greet so the participants of the camp can meet you, and then we will run the camp starting in two days and end next Saturday night with a performance at the Annex. So it is a fairly quick camp, but one I think the children attending will enjoy tremendously. I kept the camp small, as you suggested. Just six attendees, so you can provide one-on-one attention to each participant. I hope that is okay?"

Brett nodded. "That's perfect. This is the first time I've done this," he admitted, "and I would like to make this a memorable experience."

"Glenn," she called toward the back of the store.

The boy he'd noticed earlier walked up, a big smile on his face. He held out a hand, which Brett shook.

"I'm a huge fan and can't wait for the camp," he said with just the right amount of enthusiasm to set Brett's jangling nerves on end.

He hoped he could live up to the young man's expectations. The need for a drink rose strongly in his mind, but he stifled the feeling.

The dark-haired girl Glenn had been talking with before Brett had entered the store had wandered up to stand beside the boy. She looked at him, eyes wide and probably excited to be meeting a real rock star, judging by the way she paled when he reached out to shake her hand.

Her hand was tiny and smooth, and she rested it in his hand, and then quickly withdrew it.

He smiled reassuringly and said, "Are you coming to the camp, too?"

At the same time Cece said, "I've signed her up."

Meghan laughed, a slightly musical tone to her voice that was easy to listen to. "No, not me, I have no musical ability at all."

She waved her hands in denial of her attendance, and Brett shook his head. "I think you are not giving yourself full credit. You have a beautiful voice. I can hear it. Do you sing?"

"Does in the shower count?" she said with another self-deprecating laugh and shy twist of her head toward Glenn.

Glenn moved toward her, taking her hand and squeezing it. "Meghan is a little shy, but I agree, she has a beautiful voice."

Meghan laughed, laying her head on Glenn's shoulder for a second. She shifted her feet nervously and avoided looking directly at anyone.

"Hmmm . . ." was all Brett said. Then he yawned.

"Oh my," said Cece. "Forgive me, I have forgotten my manners. Glenn, do you mind driving Mr. Rhys-Falwyck up to the cabin? It's number three, and Melissa left the key under the welcome mat. Will you be returning with Glenn?"

"I think," Brett said, covering another yawn, "I probably need to at least take a nap."

Cece laughed. "I think so. I had Melissa stock the refrigerator for you, and make sure there were plenty of linens, blankets, and so on. It can get very cold up in the mountains at this time of year, of course. Although I heard we might get a thaw this week."

Brett nodded. Turning to Glenn, he said, "Ready?"

"Yep, let me get my coat, and I'll be ready."

Brett watched Glenn and Meghan walk toward the back of the store. He frowned, noticing the small studio in the corner. He walked toward the currently unoccupied room and opened the door. He admired the small setup—the equipment was very good and a surprise find in such a small town.

"People mostly use it for recording birthday greetings to family or friends, and once in a while, someone might use it for recording something more. We've had some famous musicians stop in while on vacations in the area to record a song they were inspired to write by the beauty around them."

Brett, turning to stare at her, grinned and said, "I understand the beauty part."

Cece looked at him, her blue eyes staring into his with such intensity, he lowered his own, blushing at how hokey and forward he'd sounded.

"When you are ready to come back down here, give me a call." She handed a card to him with her private number as well as the store number on it. "I live above the store and am usually down here doing something, so you can reach me at either number."

Brett looked at the card, a simple white one with gold threads twining around it to end in the shape of wings. Wings. What was going on with him? Everywhere he looked, he was back in his dream in some way, and yet wide awake.

Pocketing the card, he nodded in answer to her comment.

"How does one rent this studio?" he asked as they walked back toward the front, where Glenn waited for him. Meghan was nowhere to be seen.

"Oh, just let me know what time you want it, and I'll pencil you in," Cece answered. Looking at Glenn, she said, "You might want to let him see the town too, before you head up Burdorf Pass for the cabin."

Glenn nodded. His excitement was a tangible thing, and Brett grinned. He liked the boy. In him he could see his own youth. Brett just hoped the reality of who he was wouldn't disappoint the boy.

"Ready?" Brett clasped the boy's shoulder, squeezing slightly and then letting go.

Glenn couldn't stop grinning as he showed Brett around and gave him a brief history of the town.

"So you go to the local high school? Are you a senior?"

"Yes, I am. I play football."

"Is that what you want to do when you go to college? And then what?"

"Not sure what I want to do. I thought I might like to be a lawyer, like my dad, but not sure yet."

"I get that. So what instrument do you play?"

"Guitar." He made a turn onto a narrow road surrounded by trees. "Here we are. That was Burdorf Pass we just turned off of, and then about ten minutes up the mountain is the cabin you'll be in. It's a great cabin, by the way. I like that one best."

"Oh, how do you know?"

"In the summers, I help Melissa—Ms. Richter—maintain the cabins. I clear the brush from the winter, and my mom and sister help clean the cabins after guests have been there."

"Sounds like fun." Brett yawned again, trying hard to keep his eyes open. He wished he'd asked Glenn to stop by the coffee shop they'd passed back at the town square. Brett settled back into the seat and closed his eyes, swearing he would just need a minute to get the grit out of his eyes from being tired.

"Sir, we're here," Glenn said.

Brett felt a quick shake on his shoulder, and then the door opened, and Glenn left the car. Cold air hit Brett in the face, and he stirred.

Brett mumbled and slowly opened his eyes, gasping in surprise. He stared in pleasure at the cabin before him. It was perfect. Tucked into the forest around him, it was rustic and yet warm. Nothing prepared him for the inside, though. Expecting it to have rough wooden furniture, which would have been fine with him, instead it had thick, dark red leather couches on the first floor set in a group that encouraged conversations between guests. A large-screen TV was set over the fireplace, which had a set of logs waiting for flames. A small kitchen was off to the left as you entered, with a stove, refrigerator, and dishwasher set into dark-paneled cabinets.

Braided rugs in brilliant colors were sprinkled around the shining hardwood floors like confetti. A set of spiral stairs led to an upper loft area where he assumed was the bedroom he would be using. Another door revealed a closet, and a door at the far end of the room opened to the bathroom.

But what really drew his eye were the two French doors that led out to a back deck, where a magnificent view of the mountains rising above the forest greeted his eyes. He took in a deep breath of the pine scented air and marveled at how different it all was from the beach where he lived.

And yet, he found himself loving it just as much. Perhaps more. The sound of the waves was soothing to his soul, but this forested mountain was soothing to his mind as well.

"How odd," he mumbled.

"Odd?" said Glenn. "You don't like it?" He sounded disappointed.

"I love it." Brett breathed in deeply once more of the forest. Turning to Glenn, he said in amazement, "I've never been here before, and yet it feels like home."

Glenn chuckled. "Yeah, that's Havenwood Falls for ya. You're not the first to say that." He chuckled, as if telling a private joke.

Glenn walked back inside. Brett reluctantly followed.

"Just call me if you want to come back to town tonight. I'll come get you, but you really have quite a bit of food here. The microwave oven is behind this door." Glenn opened one of the cabinets to reveal a small microwave oven, just perfect for one-person meals or popcorn.

Once the quick tour of the place was done, Glenn left after giving Brett his phone number.

Brett watched Glenn leave, the car disappearing around the bend as if swallowed by the forest that lined both sides of the road. Shivering slightly in the cold, Brett returned inside.

Nothing in the cabin was too fancy or too over the top, and yet Brett felt it was all selected with care to provide an ambience of comfort and usability. He was surprised there was only one bedroom, but realized that was exactly perfect for his needs, so what did it matter anyway if there was only one bedroom or three?

He headed toward the fireplace and leaned down to light the logs inside, then closed the grating to keep the sparks from igniting the rug. He walked toward the kitchen, stopping at the bathroom first to splash water on his face. He was suddenly so tired, but still wanted to examine the cabin. Fighting the urge to yawn again, he checked the refrigerator. Inside were several bottles of water, sparkling water, and vitamin water. No booze, not a bottle anywhere. Hmmm . . . he remembered seeing a liquor store next to the music store.

Nope, I don't need anything strong. I just need to take a walk, he thought. *Stretching my legs might be a good idea. Keep me from wanting a drink.*

Grabbing his jacket, he set off to explore the area around the cabin. The snow was not too deep, which surprised him. He'd thought, with what the pilot had said on the plane about the new powder, that he would be knee deep in the white stuff here, too, but other than a dusting of snow in some spots, and a little deeper snow in others, the walking was easy and unencumbered by drifts.

As he walked, he noted how some of the trail looked familiar.

"That's strange," he said as he looked around. "Why do I recognize some of this?"

As he rounded a point in the trail, he stopped dead in his tracks.

Ahead of him was a large rock, a boulder, just like the one in his dreams. How was that possible?

Moving closer, Brett touched the cool rock, not surprised to find he knew the feel of it. He looked behind him quickly, half expecting the woman—Cece—to be standing there. But the trail was empty, and the trees silent.

What was happening to him? How had he ended up here, at the very cabin that was near the very rock that was part of his dreams? With the very woman serving as his hostess? Was he going crazy? He leaned his forehead against the rock, relieved that it was solid and not a figment of his imagination.

"I'm not crazy," he mumbled as he closed his eyes. "I'm not."

His only answer was a sudden wind that swirled around the boulder, picking up the snow and depositing it at his feet. He looked down, white snow covering his black boots like wings.

~

"How'd it go?" Cece asked when Glenn got back.

"Great. He's a nice guy. I like him," Glenn said. Looking around, he raised an eyebrow in puzzlement. "Where's Meghan?"

"She left. Said she had something to take care of."

"Oh." Glenn sounded disappointed, so Cece handed him a stack of CDs and pointed to the shelves.

"Can you restock these for me?"

"Sure," said Glenn flatly. He returned the vintage CDs to the shelves like a robot.

A short while later, Cece closed the store and sent Glenn home. Heading up the stairs to her apartment, she leaned against the wall when a sudden and unexpected wave of nausea overtook her.

"Not now," she said, holding her head. But there was no denying the inevitable. Sinking to the stairs, she huddled there as her mind left her body and she found herself walking in the woods again.

~

He stood, watching the woman approach. Her steps were slow and measured, her hair covering her face.

And then she looked up, met his eyes, and smiled. Her eyes were such a brilliant blue that he couldn't look away from them, could not have even said what she looked like, so trapped by her eyes was he.

"Welcome to Havenwood Falls. We are so glad you're here. There's so much you need to know."

And then she was gone, pulled from view as if she had a rope attached to her and someone had yanked her back.

He ran to where she'd been, but she was gone, not even a footprint left.

Just there, and then gone.

Welcome to Havenwood Falls, he thought.

CECE WAS SO shocked at the way that experience went that for a moment she couldn't move.

She thought about calling him, but she wasn't sure what she'd say. Should she apologize for her behavior? Explain what she meant? Did he know it was her in the dreams? She wasn't even sure what she meant. She just knew that now that he was here, she was going to have to be very careful. He was extremely vulnerable. And she had to help him, but in a way such that he wouldn't know what she was doing. And she had to keep her emotions in check. He was much more of a physical presence in person than she had expected.

Her heart, beating hard just thinking about his lean body and smile, was a dead giveaway to her reaction to him. But the darkness behind his eyes and the way the edges of his lips didn't quite complete the smile were signs of the turmoil his soul was in. He had come to her with no time to spare. Even now, she wanted to reach out to him, to hold him close and pull from him all the despair she felt flowing off him like a river of dread. His pain was her pain—she could feel it—but breaching the wall of that hurt and agony was going to take all the skill she possessed. She had a feeling he wouldn't release it easily, wouldn't let her remove it without a fight. He was clinging to it like the pain was an anchor—a reason for him to feel nothing deeply. And for a man whose words took people to heights they never expected, this was not healthy. As high as his emotions could take him, she had a feeling his valleys were equally low.

These dreams were a direct result of her emotions and her trying to reach out to heal him. With all the miles that had separated them before, there'd been no danger for her own heart. Now that he was here, within touching distance, she worried her dreams were going to become more frequent and much more . . . personal.

He was a very attractive man, and there was nothing that said they couldn't have a relationship even though she was an angel, but she wanted to be sure that she kept things on a path toward helping him heal. She needed to give him the strength to open up inside and let out what was hurting him, and then be able to move on.

But her thoughts kept returning to his eyes, those beautiful eyes in which she saw such hurt and pain, the kind that went so deep it was impossible to ignore.

BREAKING POINT

(PINK MELON: ONE TIME MORE)

Written and sung by Brett Rhys-Falwyck

Your perfume lingers in the air
but you are no longer anywhere
I thought I saw you the other day
flipping your hair in that special way

I miss your sweet smile
all promise and guile
I miss your soothing touch
that heals my heart so much

I walk the streets we used to walk
by the bench where we used to talk
Lingering there, I feel you near
even though I know you are not here

I miss your sweet smile
all promise and guile
I miss your soothing touch
that heals my heart so much

The breaking point has come and gone
Darkness closes in
Missing you is so hard to bear
I wish I just didn't care

CHAPTER 12

A knock on the door told Brett that Glenn had arrived. When he came out of the cabin, he was shivering, and Glenn chuckled.

"Cold?" he asked.

"Nope," Brett said through chattering teeth. "Just fine."

"Sure, we can go with that." Glenn chuckled. "So, you called for a trip to town?"

Brett nodded. "And coffee. Coffee shop coffee. It's always better."

"I get that," Glenn agreed, and he chatted all the way down the mountain and into town with a nervous energy Brett recognized.

After parking in the alley near the music store, the two made their way down the sidewalk and across the streets to the coffee shop.

They walked around what seemed to be the heart of the town, Glenn pointing out the shops and businesses. They passed near Whisper Falls Inn, and Glenn grinned as the owner of the inn walked onto the porch.

"Hey, Michaela," he said, waving a mittened hand. She smiled and waved before shivering and stepping back inside.

"She's pretty cool. She's with Xandru Roca. She does a lot of things around the town as the owner of the inn." They continued toward the coffee shop. "And this is Madame Tahini's, and that's Callie's Consignments. I've never been to Madame Tahini's—we have a lot of New Age stuff around here, but it's not really my thing. Callie's is cool, though. She gets vintage rock band T-shirts in all the time." As he opened the door to Coffee Haven, Glenn pointed to the shop on the other side of the coffeehouse. "And over there is Shelf Indulgence, a local bookstore—a *normal* one and not all woo-woo, like Into the Mystic by the music store. It's one of my favorite places to go, next to Coffee Haven, of course."

They ordered coffees and stepped back outside to continue their walk around the town square. Brett appreciated the tour as Glenn went on to describe some of the other shops in town, which catered to a variety of tastes. There was a shop that sold outdoors equipment and clothing for those in town for the skiing. He noticed a tattoo parlor, and Glenn wasn't exaggerating about all the New Age shops—there was one with crystals and candles and another with herbs and soaps on display in their windows. There was a jewelry store, an art studio, another coffee shop, and even a butcher shop. The two males laughed at the butcher shop's motto: "Meet Your Meat." Brett thought the town was quaint without being too touristy, and he liked it. For the first time in a long time, he felt like some of the weight he was carrying on his shoulders was lifting.

They talked a bit more as their coffee cooled in the frigid temperatures, and when Glenn dropped him back at the cabin a while later, Brett realized he'd had a great time with the young boy, and he couldn't wait to get started at the camp.

He went into the cabin, showered, and lay on the bed. He was pleasantly surprised to find how comfortable the mattress was and how exhausted he was after the tour of the town.

His last thought before sleep took him was that he liked it here.

Cece slept fitfully, his presence so close and yet so far. She could hear him breathing, his heart beating, and around him, she felt the darkness growing. A darkness she knew she had to heal before it took him over completely.

"I hope I got you here in time," she whispered to the night sky she could see through her window. The glass rattled in answer, but whether that was a good thing or not, she couldn't be sure.

There was a knocking sound. Brett sat up and looked around, taking a moment to get his bearings. He remembered where he was and that Glenn was probably at the door. Yelping a bit at the feeling of the cold floor on his bare feet, he shouted for Glenn to come in.

The door opened, and Glenn tapped his feet, knocking the snow off his boots before entering. Brett could hear the teen go to the kitchen.

Tromping down the stairs, Brett rounded the corner to the kitchen, where Glenn handed him a bag with the Coffee Haven logo on it. It smelled like warm blueberries, which could mean only one thing.

"Blueberry scones?" Brett asked with an arched eyebrow.

"I stopped there on my way here. They were just taking a batch out of the oven. I ate mine already," Glenn said with a wide smile. "Go ahead, those are for you. You cannot officially be a visitor to Havenwood Falls and not try a blueberry scone."

Brett took a bite of the sugary confection and nearly died, the taste was so delicious. He didn't even mind that it was still so warm, it burned his tongue slightly.

"Oh my God," he said with a look of euphoria on his face. "They need to franchise Coffee Haven and sell these in LA. They'd make a fortune."

He finished the whole thing while Glenn laughed. "But then why would people need to come to Havenwood Falls?"

Brett nodded in agreement. As they reached Glenn's car, he said, after taking a long swallow of the coffee, "Do we have time to stop by Coffee Haven before getting to the store? I think I might like some more of those delicious scones. They are a bit addicting."

Glenn laughed. "Your wish is my command."

The two entered Havenwood Falls Music & More a short while later with blueberry-tinged lips and full bellies. Brett thought he'd never had a more satisfying breakfast. Cece laughed at them when she caught sight of them trying to wipe the blueberry stains off their mouths.

"Where's mine?" she pretended to whine.

"I didn't forget you," Glenn said, pulling another small pouch from his pocket and handing it to her.

Brett watched Glenn stroll to the back of the store, a wide smile on his face as he greeted customers.

"Nice kid," he said, turning to face Cece.

He frowned, surprised at the expression on her face as she watched the teen at work.

"You okay?" he asked her, touching her on the arm, then jumping back slightly at the tingling in his fingertips. "What was that?" he exclaimed, examining his fingertips.

Cece pulled her arm closer to her side. "The air is so dry here in the store. Darn static electricity. And yes, Glenn is awesome. Ready to get to work? Michelle Hamlin, our local news anchor, will be here in about an hour to interview you about the camp, and then we have a few details to go over. I thought we could maybe plot out an agenda?"

"Sure." Brett rubbed his fingertips together, not sure what had just passed between them, but certain it wasn't static electricity, no matter what she said. That tingle had gone all the way to his heart, and he felt better for just having touched her.

After the interview, Ms. Hamlin promised to air the spot the next morning and also said she wouldn't miss the final performance night on Saturday. Then Cece and Brett were left alone in the store for the first time. Brett swallowed tightly.

SITTING in the back at one of the small tables where they'd held the interview, Cece watched as Michelle left, then realized she and Brett were alone. Glenn had left to run a personal errand, which probably meant he was trying to track down Meghan, who had mysteriously not been in the store so far today. With it being spring break, Cece had expected her to be here the whole day, but she hadn't put in an appearance yet.

Cece shifted in her seat at the feeling of being watched to find Brett looking at her with a puzzled expression. He was trying to figure something out, and Cece had a feeling she knew what it was.

"So," she said, surprised at how nervous she felt. The store was eerily quiet, and she prayed for a customer to walk through the door to alleviate some of the silence.

"So," Brett repeated. He leaned closer to her, and she could smell the musky cologne he wore that was tinged with an orangey smell. She found herself lost in his scent and had to pull herself back mentally by shifting her position in the chair slightly.

The sound of the chair scraping against the floor made her jump.

Brett had stood up, his back tight and straight. She wondered if he felt the same tension she did. She waited for him to speak, not wanting to break into his thoughts.

"What about this recording studio? Do you mind if I look at it?"

"Not at all," Cece said. Happy to have something to do, she walked toward the front. "Let me get the key."

She returned a moment later. As she handed him the key, she accidently touched his hand, and the images that flooded into her mind were dark and sad. She gasped before grabbing the back of a chair as her knees weakened slightly. When she'd regained her breath, she reached out, her fingers gently brushing against Brett's skin along his wrist as she attempted to pull some of the darkness from him and replace it with something more pleasant. At first she felt she was succeeding, but then a tingling went back up her arm as she felt something transfer from him to her. There was a rustling sound as a small, dark whisper entered her mind.

I am coming, and you cannot stop me this time. The voice was venomous and evil.

And she knew who it was.

She knew what was holding the darkness in Brett.

She grasped the cross on her chest as she fought to simply breathe.

INSIDE THE DARKNESS

(BRETT RHYS-FALWYCK SOLO ALBUM: OCEANS)

Written and sung by Brett Rhys-Falwyck

I am a lonely bird flying high
You cannot hear me sigh
I am calling out for you
but on winged promise you flew

Inside the darkness we all fear
nothing reaches us, we're
adrift on the hopeless sea
in a world that's forgotten peace

Reaching, clawing, scratching to get out
I cannot leave the feelings behind, doubt
creeps in like a monster under the bed
inside my heart, inside my head

Inside the darkness we all fear
nothing reaches us, we're
adrift on the hopeless sea
in a world that's forgotten peace

Find me, bring me to the light
Keep me in the day, not the night
I don't want to be without you
for to live that way is a life untrue

Inside the darkness we all fear
nothing reaches us, we're
adrift on the hopeless sea
in a world that's forgotten peace

CHAPTER 13

*I*n spite of his resolve to remain cool, Brett felt his heart pounding in his chest. There was something about this woman that was making it hard for him to breathe. She was calming and exciting at the same time, like no one he'd ever met before. He felt something inside break away when she touched him. Something that was small and dark and hurtful, and he didn't understand it, but he felt a desire to crush her in his embrace.

But why? He'd never felt this way before. And then the feeling was gone from him, and he was left shaking, like he was in some weird kind of detox.

Checking out the studio seemed the safest way to be away from her, but he hadn't counted on the narrowness of the room. The equipment was good, not top of the line, but good enough for what she had it there for, and reminded him of the equipment he'd seen in the radio station at college where he'd spent some nights spinning records and romancing Lucy Albertson, the night-shift DJ.

He hadn't gotten anywhere with Lucy, but he had discovered a love for anything music, and recording equipment was his jam. He loved playing with the buttons and knobs and trying to find the right sound for the right moment in a song. He loved the purity of bringing a note from a guitar, but didn't mind getting into the studio and manipulating some weird blends when they were recording.

"What do you think?" Cece asked, stepping into the room with him. She stood close enough that he could hear her breathing, and he shoved his hands in his pants pockets to keep from reaching out for her.

She'd given him the quick instructions on the equipment and how to use it, and even though he didn't need them, he listened carefully, his attention fully on her.

Glenn came back a few minutes later, his expression sad, and informed them he couldn't find Meghan.

"Oh, she'll be by when she can," Cece said with confidence. "She's probably doing something for her mom."

Glenn nodded and went back to work.

CECE POINTED to the door of the store. "Would you like to get something for lunch? We have a decent pizza place. Napoli's is just a little ways across the square. Care to join me?"

"Love to. I just had some scones, but there's always room for pizza," said Brett. "Should we see if Glenn wants anything?"

"Oh, I already know what he'll want. A personal pizza with everything on it, right Glenn?"

Glenn nodded, but without enthusiasm. Cece studied him for a minute, but he refused to turn around.

"Let me get my coat. Glenn, will you watch the store?"

"Sure," Glenn said. "I have nothing else to do."

Cece hugged him. "She'll be here. Be patient."

When they got to Napoli's, the lunch crowd was just leaving, so they were able to snag a table in the back. Cece moved the green tablecloth around and smoothed it out, her OCD showing, which made Brett chuckle.

They placed their orders and silence descended.

"So, what do you think of Havenwood Falls so far?" she asked, trying to make conversation to cover the awkward silence.

She studied him while he twirled his empty water glass. His eyes were a magnificent green, with lashes girls would pay a fortune to buy at the makeup counter. His nose was long and slender, but not overly large. His lips, though, were fantastic—full and round—and she felt herself wanting to wipe a drop of water beading on the center of the bottom lip.

"I think this place is named quite well. I could certainly *fall* for this *haven* in the *woods*."

"Yep." Cece laughed. "That's what a lot of people say."

"Why have I never heard of it before?" Brett asked her, his eyes trapping hers, as if waiting for her to lie.

"Because we value our town just as it is," Cece said after a moment's thought. "It is a place people come to, and then leave. We like it that way."

"Ah, so come and spend your money, but take your life's tragedies, and stories, and dramas home with you."

"Something like that," Cece agreed, before taking a sip of her water even though she wasn't thirsty. "But not in quite that cynical of a tone," she admonished him softly.

"Sorry," Brett mumbled as their order arrived.

Conversation stalled as they finished their meal. Cece insisted on paying, telling him it was part of the expenses for running the camp.

They hurried back to the store with Glenn's lunch, and when

they returned, they found the store bustling with teens, all of whom wanted to meet Brett. He greeted his fans with a grace any politician would envy as he chatted with them, signed whatever they put in front of him, and told them to be sure to come to the performance on Saturday night at the Annex.

"Ms. Amundson?" said a girl standing at her elbow. "I'm Zoey. I cannot wait for the camp to begin. What time do I need to be here?"

Cece handed the girl a packet she'd prepared for the camp and then called Glenn to the front. Handing him the rest of the packets, she asked him to give them out to any of the other camp members who might be there.

She saw Kase chatting with Elle Martin, or maybe chatting wasn't the right word. It was much more like flirting, and she smiled, watching their innocent banter. *That's what love should be like,* Cece thought.

"Penny for your thoughts," said Brett at her side.

"Hardly worth it," Cece said with a grin.

Brett's eyes darkened for just a moment, and she felt herself drawn into him. The pull of his physicality was so strong, she felt her breath catch and put her hands at her sides to keep from reaching out to touch him.

"I need to step outside for a minute," Cece said. She rushed out the door and around the corner, standing on the side of the building while breathing hard.

Looking up, she whispered, "I don't know what you want. I don't know what you expect me to do. Guide me."

But there was nothing.

"Ms. Amundson?" said a male voice from behind her.

Cece turned to see Laine standing there with a nearly unconscious Meghan in his arms. He was holding her up, his hands on her upper arms all that were keeping her from falling to the ground. There was blood on her face, and a gash on her lip that was slowly oozing dark blood. Blood way too dark to be from a simple wound.

Cece grabbed Meghan before she fell when Laine let her go.

"I didn't mean to do it," he sobbed. "I don't know how it happened."

In his eyes, Cece saw fear, as if he had done something he couldn't fix.

"Meghan!" Glenn was at her side in two seconds and shoving Laine into the street.

"What did you do? What did you *do*? I'll kill you for this." Glenn threw his fists up, and Cece, unable to intervene because of the girl in her arms, watched in horror as Glenn went for the other boy.

And then, when it seemed the two would come to blows, for Laine had put up his arms in defense against the forthcoming attack, Glenn was lifted off his feet and set backwards. Brett stood between them.

"How about we take this off the street, and you gentlemen both come inside, and we'll figure out what happened? Glenn, you first."

Glenn, his face angry and red, moved toward the door, casting evil glances back at Laine the whole time.

"Laine, you next. Glenn, you go to that corner. Laine over there. Everyone else? Thank you for coming by, but please leave now. Show's over."

The kids dispersed quickly, and Cece marveled at how easily Brett was able to gain control of the situation. In her arms, Meghan moaned.

Zoey, looking at Meghan with concern, said, "Can I help?"

"Yes, thank you, Zoey. Would you get Dr. Underwood?"

Zoey was gone and Dr. Underwood was at the shop in no time to bandage Meghan's wounds. She hadn't said a word to anyone about what had happened, and while she was being cared for—a few quick patches on the deeper wound and she was good—the boys glared at each other.

Dr. Underwood left, declining payment and saying he wanted to get out for some coffee anyway and check to see if there were still any blueberry scones to be had. Once the door closed behind him, Brett looked at the two boys and then Meghan, and sighed.

"Someone had better talk, or I am going to draw my own conclusions," said Brett when the silence seemed to stretch on forever.

"What did you do to Meghan?" growled Glenn, his eyes daggers of hate.

"He didn't do anything," Meghan said with a great sigh. She was shaking, and Cece moved closer to her to see if the girl was cold. "He was helping me."

"Helping you? What happened?"

"I don't want to talk about it," Meghan said with lowered eyes.

"Meghan," said Glenn softly as he moved toward her, "you can tell us. No matter what happened, you can tell us about it."

"I . . . I fell?"

"Did you fall?" Brett asked, the disbelief in his tone reflecting Cece's feelings.

"Meghan, you'd better tell them the truth, or I think Glenn might jump me in a dark alley," Laine said.

Glenn looked over at Laine, who just shrugged.

"I don't blame you," Laine said to Glenn. "If I had a great girlfriend like Meghan, I would fight for her, too."

"I was walking over here," Meghan said, "and I walked by the mouth of an alley, and there were some guys in there. They grabbed me and told me to give them my money, but I didn't have enough, so they started pushing me. I slipped on the ice and fell, and then Laine saw them, and he got me out of there."

"Who were they?" Cece asked in alarm, her eyes immediately going outside.

"I don't know. They didn't look familiar, and it was dark in the alley. I didn't really see them. I was too scared to look."

"I figured I should bring her here first. I wasn't sure where else to go with her," Laine said.

"You did the right, Laine," Cece reassured him. "Thank you for being there and for helping Meghan."

"Yeah, thank you," said Glenn reluctantly when Cece tossed him a look.

Glenn got up, and with a look at both Cece and Brett, he advanced toward Laine with his hand out.

"Thank you," he said more sincerely.

"I think Meghan needs to go home," Cece said, standing. "Glenn, will you take Laine and Meghan home? I think I need to talk to Sheriff Kasun about this attack on you, Meghan, so he might want to talk to you later. But for now, I think going home is the best medicine we can give you."

The three teens nodded, and Glenn left with his arm around Meghan's shoulder. The look that passed between the two boys walking on either side of Meghan was both territorial and friendly.

Cece called Sheriff Kasun, who stopped by a short while later to get her report. She asked him not to talk to Meghan until tomorrow.

"Give her time to recover," she begged him, and he nodded agreement.

Sheriff Kasun thanked Cece for the information and promised to find the perpetrators and let her know when he did. Cece nodded and showed him out, locking the door behind the sheriff.

Then she realized she and Brett were alone again. She cleared her throat. "Shall we work on the agenda? Or would you like to get some dinner?"

"Dinner? What time is it?"

"Six."

"Already? Dinner, then," Brett said as his stomach suddenly rumbled loud enough that both of them heard it.

THEY DECIDED to have dinner at the country club. Walking with the town lit up with twinkling lights on the shops and buildings, Brett couldn't help but feel like he was in a fairy tale.

All we need now, he thought, *is the big bad wolf.*

QUICKER THAN MY HEARTBEAT

(BONUS TRACK, BRETT RHYS-FALWYCK SOLO ALBUM: OCEANS)

Written and sung by Brett Rhys-Falwyck

I held the heart of a woman
until I let it go
Held it close and tight
until I let it go

She trusted me with her greatest treasure
and I lost it
She warned me of the ways this would go
and I lost it

Quicker than my heartbeat she was gone
never seen again
I looked for her in all the places, but she was
never seen again

I lost my reason, I lost my mind
once upon a time
The fairytale love story was over
once upon a time

CHAPTER 14

"**W**ell, would you like to come in for some cocoa?" Cece offered when they returned to the store later that evening. Unlocking the door, she looked over her shoulder to see Brett staring off into the distance with a wistful look on his face. Her breath caught at how beautiful he was.

His melancholy was a dark shadow on his soul. She could feel it in his every breath, how that despair was slowly spreading through his body. Every deep moment was giving him over to the darkness. She needed to fill his life with light and love and happiness if she was to save him.

Too late, you're too late. I've found you. It won't be long now. My retribution will come. You will pay. You will all pay.

Cece shivered as Brett turned to look at her. In his eyes, she saw something burning, something dark and not human. And then it was gone, and she wondered if she saw it at all when he smiled at her.

"Hey," he said, "cocoa sounds like the perfect ending to a really awesome day."

Cece smiled, opened the door, and ushered him in ahead of her.

Walking up the stairs, she led Brett to her humble apartment. It was sparse, with barely any furniture and wood floors that gleamed from her weekly cleanings. A sofa, large and comfortable, sat on a braided rug in a multitude of reds, blues, and yellows, her favorite colors—red for love, blue for faith, and yellow for sunshine.

She had a bookcase filled to overflowing with so many books and a small flat-screen TV set in a corner. Cece led him to the dining room and invited him to sit in one of the four chairs at the small table. A bedroom was to the left of the dining room, where colorful quilts rested on her bed. There was a dresser and a small bathroom farther into the room. Fluffy pillows and shams decorated the bed in solids of red, blue, and yellow, a recurring theme in the décor.

Off to the right of the dining room was a small kitchen with a refrigerator, stove, and dishwasher, along with several floor-to-ceiling cabinets in dark wood. Yellow curtains covered the two windows, one over the sink and the other near the last set of cabinets. They faced the street.

Rather than taking the seat she'd offered, Brett followed her into the kitchen.

"Marshmallows?" he asked when they were done with the cocoa preparations and the beverage was cooling in tall mugs with pictures of puppies on them.

"Top shelf, third cabinet," Cece responded, taking their cups into the other room.

BRETT FOUND the marshmallows and grabbed the bag. Sitting across from her in the dining room, he occupied his time stirring his cocoa and squirting on whipped cream while sneaking glances at her.

With fine-boned cheeks and a pretty upturned nose, she had

bright gray-blue eyes and a small bow-shaped mouth that made him think of how nice it would be to kiss her.

"So," Cece said, putting her cup on the table after taking one sip. "What do you want to do tomorrow?"

"Ski?" Brett said, remembering the conversation on the plane and wanting, for his own satisfaction, to prove the old lady wrong.

"Hmmm . . . I haven't skied in a while, but I suppose we can try it."

"We?"

"Sure, I'll come with you," she said casually. "Can't have you falling and breaking your neck or slamming into a tree."

"Great," Brett said, and he meant it. He found his heart quickening at the thought of skiing with her by his side. He envisioned them gracefully gliding from the top of the mountain to the bottom without falling even once.

"Have you skied before?" Cece asked.

"Um . . . no, but how hard can it be?" Brett said confidently.

Cece chuckled. "It's not the skiing that's hard. It's the landing."

Brett gulped, pretending it was because the cocoa was hot. He glanced up at her, and they both burst into laughter.

Her laugh, Brett thought, a lump in his chest lightening a little, *is amazing.*

Then he felt his chest tighten again, and he had to look away. His hand gripped the mug so hard, he thought he might break the ceramic, but he couldn't let go. It was burning his hand, but he was unable to release the mug.

Cece was at his side in a second. She put her hand, cool and smooth, on his and whispered something he couldn't quite catch, and his hand finally, reluctantly released the mug.

"I'm sorry," Brett whispered. "I'm not sure what happened. I couldn't let it go."

"It's okay." Cece's voice was soothing, and Brett felt himself relaxing. He leaned into her shoulder and in seconds felt himself drifting off.

"I'm not sure what's wrong with me," he whispered into her hair, which smelled of jasmine and summertime. "I'm so tired."

Just before Morpheus claimed him, Brett thought he heard her whisper, her breath like the flutter of a butterfly's wing on his cheek, "Sleep now, my dream lover," but before he could ask her what she'd said, his eyes closed, and he remembered nothing else.

He was there again, only this time he didn't remember walking.

Looking around the clearing, he saw the rock glinting silver in the moonlight.

She stood next to him, and any doubts he'd had before were gone. She was definitely Cece.

He had wings, just like hers, only they were a soft light gray while hers were brilliant white.

He reached for her, and she took his hand, and then suddenly the sky overhead, which had been blue and perfect just moments before, became dark. Lightning shot through it, and his hand in hers tightened even as she tried to free herself.

She whimpered like a bird caught in the jaws of a tiger.

He looked around wildly, trying to let her go, but unable to break the connection.

She was his, no one else's, and he wasn't going to let her go.

He felt his eyes roll back in his head. His beautiful white gown became blood red, and his wings, his beautiful gray wings, became black. No, not black. They were darker than black, shot through with blood-red lines that pulsed and throbbed and . . . lived. They lived.

He felt himself turning to her, a grin so wide it split his face.

"I'm back, darling. Did you miss me?"

And then his mouth opened wide, and he screamed, a horrible scream, the pain so great he felt himself falling out of himself.

Then he heard the scream, and the sound of bones breaking, and—

"SHHH . . . Brett, it's okay, it's okay. It's gone. The dream is gone. You're okay. You're okay."

Brett opened his eyes slowly, afraid to look, afraid to see if he'd hurt her.

"What's happening to me?"

Cece didn't answer. She just kept rocking him until he fell back to sleep, to dream no more that night.

In the darkness, she heard a deep laugh that chilled her to the very bone.

How could he have found me here? I was so careful.

CLARITY

(BRETT RHYS-FALWYCK SOLO ALBUM: OCEANS)

Written and sung by Brett Rhys-Falwyck

In between yesterday and today
there lies a twist of fate
a moment of clarity
that makes time still

where choices don't matter
decisions aren't made
lives don't change
nothing bad happens

When time rolls around again
clarity is lost to reality
payments come due
good and bad are battles

Winning doesn't mean you win
Losing doesn't mean you lose
Choices don't mean you choose
Clarity takes away all doubt

CHAPTER 15

*B*rett woke in a strange bed and found Cece lying next to him. His mouth was as dry as a desert, and he knew he must not only stink, but his breath must smell worse than a skunk in heat.

Covering his mouth, he breathed into his hand and grimaced. Yeah, maybe two skunks in heat. Both without having had a bath in a month.

Lying back into the pillow, he stared up at the ceiling and wondered why he felt like he'd run a marathon or two. His body was exhausted, and he hadn't done anything. At least, he thought he hadn't. He pulled his waistband away from his skin and groaned. Nope, he hadn't done anything.

How had he let a whole night slip by in a beautiful woman's bed, without trying to take advantage of her? How had that happened?

He carefully rolled off the bed, relieved to find his boots were still by the door. He would slip downstairs and out of the store before Glenn or anyone else got here. He'd sneak out and get them both coffee and act like he hadn't just spent the night with her without having *spent the night* with her. What kind of reputation would he get after this? A rock star and a beautiful angel like her, and he didn't try to bed her?

Craziness.

And then, looking at her beautiful face in slumber, he thought, *I could climb right back in that bed and right that wrong pretty quickly*. But then he stopped. She looked so beautiful, he just couldn't stand to wake her.

This must be how Prince Charming felt looking at Sleeping Beauty, he thought, *except I am no Prince Charming, Disney version or not.* He was so caught up in his thoughts, he missed when she woke.

"Hey," he said, "sorry about being such a lousy house guest. Fell asleep."

Cece rose from the bed in one fluid movement that stilled his heart, it was so beautiful. "No worries, I could see you were exhausted and thought you might like the bed instead of the couch. You are a little too tall for my couch."

She smiled.

How can she look so beautiful first thing in the morning? Most women he knew needed hours to get ready to face the day, but here she was, looking like she'd just been to a spa and gotten the works done. Her skin was translucent, like pearls, it was so clear and white. Her hair looked like she'd just finished brushing it, with only a few strands out of place. Most women he saw in the morning had hair like rats had slept in it after a night with him, and yet she was magazine-model perfect.

"How do you do it?" he whispered to her in awe.

"Do what?" she asked, confused about the question.

"Look so perfect first thing in the morning?"

She laughed.

"Breakfast?" she asked, ignoring his question.

She walked to the bathroom and closed the door. He heard water running and the toilet flushing, and then she returned. She'd changed her clothes into a different pair of jeans and a soft pink plaid shirt that complemented her skin perfectly.

She slipped on her boots, and he followed her downstairs.

"I have to wait for Glenn to get here, but then we can go to Coffee Haven and get some of that delicious brew and hopefully some scones fresh out of the oven."

"That sounds like heaven," Brett said with a deep chuckle, appreciating her idea for breakfast one hundred percent.

Glenn walked in and grumbled a greeting.

"You okay, Glenn?" Cece asked, concern for her teen employee causing a set of lines to appear between her brows.

"I'm good, sorry. Had to talk to Sheriff Kasun until around eleven last night. He says they're gonna catch the guys who did that to Meghan, but I don't know. They could be anywhere by now."

"Oh, I think you need to trust Rusty and Sheriff Kasun. No matter where those guys go, they'll find them. You know how they are about protecting the town. No gangs, no thugs, no troublemakers—that's their motto."

"Yeah, I guess so." Glenn didn't sound convinced.

"You let the sheriff and his people handle this, Glenn," said Cece seriously. She locked eyes with him. "They'll get them."

Glenn nodded. "Where are you guys off to so early? Oh, sorry I didn't run you back to the cabin last night, Brett," Glenn said. "I forgot."

"All good," Brett said. "I understand. You had more important things to deal with. I was fine."

"Good," Glenn said, not seeming to realize that Brett had spent the night with his boss. Or just not caring.

Either way, Brett was relieved he didn't have to defend Cece's honor.

"Coffee, scones? Let's go. Glenn, you're good here until we get back?"

Glenn nodded, already going around the store and restacking items that had been messed up yesterday.

Coffee and scones in hand—they were lucky enough to catch a batch just out of the oven—Cece and Brett walked around. Cece took him to get some ski clothes, and Brett was ready for the adventure.

"You'll have to change at the lodge. They have lockers you can put your clothes in when you change. That okay?

Brett nodded. He looked up the mountain and smiled. He'd always wanted to learn to ski. He thought it looked like a lot of fun.

An hour later, he wondered why he ever thought hurtling down a mountain, at God knows how many miles an hour with only two sticks on his feet and flimsy aluminum poles in his hands, would be fun. He held his breath and tried not to close his eyes as trees rushed past him at abnormal speeds.

This boy, he told himself, *is never doing this again, no matter how much it might impress the girl.*

When he limped his way back to the lodge, he was not surprised to see that Cece was an expert. She was helping a little girl who was taking the bunny hill course like a champ, but got stuck where the snow had drifted up, and her ski went in point first.

The mound of snow was slightly icy, and the ski was definitely stuck. Brett limped over, setting his skis down next to the observation area where parents stood while their children took lessons. He grabbed hold of Cece's waist, and she grabbed hold of the little girl's waist, and slowly walking backward, they were able to free the little girl. Just as Brett stood to raise his hands in a victory salute, his foot caught on some ice, and he started to fall.

Cece, seeing what was about to happen, grabbed him in an effort to help him keep on his feet, but instead, both of them fell. She landed on top of him, hard enough to take away his breath.

"Well," Brett said with a lascivious wink. "I love when the woman takes the top."

Cece's eyes grew wide, and her mouth parted to say something back, but Brett, overcome by blueberry scones (he would claim later that they were an aphrodisiac), kissed her.

As his lips claimed hers, he thought, *I know these lips,* and he felt her body press into his as she kissed him back with just as much passion.

"Uh, folks, you want to take that to a room?"

Brett broke the kiss as Cece rolled off him. Gaining his feet, he nodded as the crowd around them clapped their approval.

"This is the kiddie hill. You want to romance your girl," the pimply faced kid with the yellow guard badge on his sleeve said, "there's cabins at the lodge you can rent."

Heads down and holding hands, Brett and Cece ran through the crowd to collapse laughing against some trees lining the walkway to the lodge.

Brett's lips were still tingling as they made their way down the street to the square. As they walked to the shop, neither spoke. Brett was still puzzled by how familiar her kiss had felt to him, but didn't know what to say about it. Or if he should even say anything. Would she think she was being compared to other women and found wanting? Or worse yet, would she think he thought she was just like everyone else? That was so far from the case that he wondered about that too.

"Penny for your thoughts," Cece teased as they stepped into the warm interior of the shop. Customers were perusing the stacks, and Glenn was chatting with Laine as if they were old friends.

Seeing them enter the shop, Glenn broke away and hurried toward them.

"You just missed Sheriff Kasun. He said to give you this."

Glenn handed Cece an envelope on which her name was scrawled.

"Excuse me," she said, taking the envelope and disappearing up the stairs.

~

ONCE SHE GOT into her apartment, Cece opened the envelope with shaking fingers.

Cece –
You know the rules.
Court of the Sun and the Moon
9pm tonight
Don't be late.
SK
P.S. we caught them. A couple demons out for some fun. All taken care of.

"Well," she whispered to the empty room as she tapped the letter against her chin, "at least they saved me the trouble of contacting them, but how did they know?"

Those demons who attacked Meghan had not done it randomly. They'd gone after someone she knew, and they'd done it on someone's orders. She knew this as surely as she knew Sheriff Kasun hadn't wanted things to go this far. He'd warned her —told her that she needed to handle her own shit or the Court would.

Well, now it was in the Court's hands what happened to her. She could only hope the benefit of the doubt would land on her side.

She wanted to stay in Havenwood Falls. She had a feeling she had more to do and leaving now would not be in the best interests of the town.

But how could she convince them that she had not invited Gregoire here, that his being here was not her fault?

"Well, girl," she told herself sternly, "you'd better figure out a way, or you're in big trouble."

CECE FINALLY CAME DOWNSTAIRS and asked Glenn if he could drive Brett to the cabin, telling them both she had something she had to do tonight and wouldn't be available.

Brett, realizing Cece wasn't going to let him stay the night again, cursed the letter she'd received. One benefit of the letter, though, was finding out that the gang that had attacked Meghan had been caught and was no longer in town.

Glenn, his face set in a stern line, didn't keep it secret that he still wanted to find them and beat the living tar out of them, but Cece wisely counseled him that even if he did find them, and even if he and Laine both tried to take care of it on their own, there were still more members of that gang than the two of them could handle.

"Meghan's fine. A little shook up, as we all are, but she's made a full recovery, and she'll be good. So no harm, no foul, and the guys are gone," Cece said.

Grumbling, Glenn and Laine agreed, but still wanted to take out their anger on them.

"Forget it," Brett advised them. "Cece's right. Nothing will come of any more violence, other than someone else might get hurt, and might get hurt worse. We let it go. Agreed?"

With great sighs, as if Brett had asked them to clean their rooms, they both agreed to let it go.

"Now," Brett said to Cece, "what's this about you going someplace after dark in a town with thugs like these around? At least let me go with you, wherever it is."

CECE DECLINED BRETT'S kind offer and once again asked Glenn to run Brett and Laine home. Glenn grabbed his keys and coat and told them both to head to his car.

"You sure you'll be okay, boss?"

She nodded, keeping worry from her face, lest he see it. "Yep, I'll be fine."

She kept the smile plastered on her face until she saw Glenn's car leave. Then she collapsed against the wall and took a few shaky breaths until she felt her pounding heart calm.

"I cannot tell a lie," she said to the empty store, "but I might have just stretched the truth a little thin."

Looking around the store, a place she'd come to love and enjoy working in, she headed upstairs to change before meeting with the Court to decide her fate.

Would they let her stay?

Would they offer help?

Or would they tell her to leave, knowing the kind of chaos Gregoire could wreak?

JUDGMENT

(BRETT RHYS-FALWYCK YOUTUBE SINGLE)

Written and sung by Brett Rhys-Falwyck

A right must be avenged
Darkness must be revenged
A curse must be lifted
A talent must be gifted

Old meets new in a flash of light
Tomorrow becomes yesterday's night
The world twists upside down
for the girl in snow-white gown

A celestial judgment fixes all wrongs
A lover must leave where he doesn't belong
A heart lies wasted
too broken to be pasted

Adrift on a sea of forgetting
a lover seeks a last kiss, letting
it linger until time passes on
and the insatiable need is gone

Time takes its due
Me without you
Hearts beat again
Memory wanes

CHAPTER 16

$\mathcal{U}$nder cover of night, Cece left her store, and huddled inside a cloak, she made her way carefully down the block, past several storefronts now closed, as it was almost nine, and around the square until she faced City Hall.

Going around to the back of the structure, she found the door. A small sliver of light was revealed as she stepped inside. Her feet sounded hollow as she walked down the hallway to the room for the meeting she was being summoned to. No one was nearby, and the building felt narrow and confining. She wished, for just a moment, that she could free her wings and fly into the meeting.

That would be spectacular, she thought. *Would they let me in? Would they be impressed to see me in all my angelic glory? Probably not,* she decided. *They see supernaturals for what they are. I would be just one of many, since they are mostly supernaturals themselves.*

She slowed her steps, breathing in and out in a conscious effort to calm her racing nerves.

The Court knew her story. A supernatural couldn't be in Havenwood Falls and not be known to the Court, so she wasn't sure why she'd been summoned so harshly. As an angel, she was more powerful than anyone on the Court, which put her beyond their reach, but she didn't want to test them like that. Ever since she'd come to town, she'd wanted only to be a blessing and a friend to them. What had she done wrong?

You know what they want. You know what happens if you give it to them.

She shivered, then straightened. Her story was not much different than anyone else's, and she kept repeating that to herself in case any of the Court members were reading her mind. She metaphorically shoved that dark voice into a filing cabinet and slammed the door closed. She would *not* allow them to read her. She would *not* allow them to invade her privacy. Thoughts of Brett intruded, and she pushed them away. She could not let them know what he was coming to mean to her.

"I am stronger than I look," she whispered before opening the door to the room where the members of the Court waited for her. She heard the faint bongs of a clock striking nine as she entered. "I am stronger . . ."

Her voice faded into silence as she saw each face rise up to meet her gaze.

Oh shit, she thought, *I'm as weak as a kitten.* It took all her willpower to walk into that room and not take wing and fly away. *That would serve them right,* she thought, keeping her face straight. *If I did fly out of here they probably wouldn't know what to do.*

And then a voice intruded, gruff and old. *The room is charmed, dear. You can't fly, but I don't blame you for wanting to.*

She snapped around, trying to decide who had spoken, but all the faces greeting her were solemn and serious. Not one looked like someone who would have invaded her mind.

She hoped they wouldn't send her away. She'd come to love this place in her short time here. She'd made friends and was happy. Havenwood Falls was her home, and her heart was here.

Elsmed Fairchild, a member of the court, pointed to a chair.

She sat, fully understanding his meaning. "No need to be afraid, dear. We just need to have a friendly little chat."

Somehow Cece had a feeling that was not quite the truth. A chat with the Court usually held consequences. There was nothing friendly about their chats, in her experience. Of course, she'd only sat in this room once before, upon her arrival, when the town's rules were explained to her and Addie had given her the small halo tattoo that graced her ankle.

As an angel, it had seemed appropriate at the time, and periodically she considered having a second tattoo added, but had so far kept her skin unmarked any more.

Cece looked at the faces of the Court, all people she knew from town. She nodded to Sheriff Kasun, who didn't acknowledge her gesture at first, but then winked, oh so slowly, and she smirked in response. Always stern, it was amusing to see him let his guard down for those few seconds, and she appreciated his attempt to put her at ease.

There were a couple of empty seats, she noted, but it appeared they had a quorum, or perhaps, since they were just having a "friendly chat," they didn't need everyone there. She wasn't sure what to expect, and folded her hands in her lap. Taking a deep breath, she waited for them to begin.

Sheriff Kasun cleared his throat, stood, and looking at everyone, said, "I asked for the Court to meet regarding the strange assault on the human girl, Meghan Gonzalez, by four teens whom later we found to be demons."

Cece looked over at Ric, hoping his explanation would be enough to save her from too much trouble.

He continued, avoiding her eyes. "The girl was attacked in the mouth of an alley not far from the music store Cecelia," he waved in her direction, "owns and runs. We believe the girl was headed over there and was attacked as she walked past. The demons who attacked her were apprehended, and the girl is okay. She suffered a few cuts and a bloody nose, but was otherwise unharmed. We don't believe the intent was to hurt the girl . . . this time. Upon questioning the demons, we discovered they were the only ones who managed to enter through a portal. They were disguised within students, part of a group who came here to ski."

The Court members looked at each other in surprise. Their wards should have prevented this breach. Saundra Beaumont and Mathilde Augustine, two of the three leaders of the Luna Coven, which was responsible for the wards, asked a few questions of Sheriff Kasun.

His frustration began to show. "We think they had possessed the bodies of these teens and then forced them to do this. We also believe they would have been unable to maintain their forms much longer. Two of the demons we were able to separate from the teens dissolved into dust as we questioned them. The other two dissolved a short while later. We videoed our interview and caught them as they disappeared into thin air. Even the dust from their bodies disappeared. It was strange, but they are gone. Rusty, Conall, and the rest of my men have been checking the boundaries to see if we sense anything else, but there are no other demons that have not been categorized or registered. We believe it was a one-time event and that there are no others around to be worried about. We think they were part of a lesser group of demons, called Berith, known to cause mischief. They are not in any way associated with any of the demons currently in town."

Sheriff Kasun returned to his seat and waited for more questions to come. For the next fifteen minutes, he was grilled about the demons and his ideas for why they were there. He handled the questions with his usual grace, answering everything they threw at him.

"Bottom line is they're gone, and I found no others in town," he said, keeping the annoyance out of his tone, though barely.

Cece admired his aplomb and wished she felt as sure of her own part, but her heart was pounding in her chest, and she marveled that no one heard it.

Elsmed looked over at Cece once the questions for Sheriff Kasun stopped.

"And what do you think?"

"I . . . I'm not really sure what you need from me," Cece said truthfully.

"How do you think the demons got here?" The ancient fae leaned toward her, and Cece had the impression that his anger was only being held under control by sheer force of will. He might have been ancient, but he was no fool. She wondered if he could sense her fear, her uncertainty.

"I . . ." Cece licked her lips.

"They didn't mention Cece at all," Sheriff Kasun interjected. Every head on the Court swiveled in his direction, even Elsmed's, although he was the last to look at the wolf-shifter lawman.

"That doesn't excuse her from questions, Ric. You know that." Saundra looked at Cece. Her eyes softened slightly, and Cece relaxed, praying it wouldn't be too horrible. "Due to your previous encounters with demons and our own experience last Thanksgiving, it is only natural that we might like to question you and the other angels in town about these Berith. You understand, don't you?"

"I don't know anything about these demons," Cece started to say before Elsmed interrupted her.

"But you know about demons, don't you, Cecelia Eurydice Amundson? Don't you?" He whispered the last two words, and she shivered.

Just how much did they know, or did they infer, about her story from the one she told them when she arrived?

Cece purposely kept her mind blank, away from thoughts of Gregoire Penumbra, the reason she'd come to Havenwood Falls in the first place. She slammed that cabinet drawer shut when she felt the gentle tug that meant someone here was trying to read her mind.

"I know about demons," Cece said with a firmness that showed her sincerity. "I am an angel, after all. As Saundra just pointed out."

A few titters came from the other members of the Court, and Elsmed sent them a warning look, which silenced them, but Cece noticed a few were smirking when he looked back to her.

She met the fae's gaze squarely, refusing to back down. She had nothing to hide, nothing to explain. Nothing to fear . . . she hoped.

"What was the name of the town you lived in before coming here?"

She stilled. His frosty blue eyes were boring into her, and she looked down.

"I came here from a small town in Montana. I think it should be in my file, or whatever record you use to keep track of your visitors and residents." She tried to keep her voice even, to not let him know how he was affecting her.

Ric shifted in his seat, but didn't interfere. Perhaps he had been burned too many times by the fae to get involved.

Cece was careful to keep her eyes only on Elsmed.

"If I remember correctly from your . . . *file* . . ." He stretched out the word in response to her comment, but she did not react. He continued, "You came to us because you had battled a demon and needed a place to hide from him. Is that correct?"

Cece nodded.

"You can see how we might need to question you about these teen demons after your previous encounter with a demon. Your connection to the girl who was attacked makes it a possibility that you might somehow be part of this intrusion."

Cece shook her head. "I have no idea who those demons were. They didn't get in contact with me, and I don't know of any reason they might have attacked someone I knew. The demon I battled with before coming to Havenwood Falls could not have been here.

Surely your wards would have stopped him, and I haven't had any contact with him since I last saw him."

That part was true, she consoled herself. After all, she'd only heard him—she hadn't actually seen him—and the voice might not even have been his. It could have all just been her imagination.

"Have you asked Harper or Elias if they know anything?" Cece asked, referring to the psychic scribe who channeled dark spirts and demons, and a fallen angel who lived in town.

"They had no knowledge of their presence," Ric said.

"I have nothing to help you, either," Cece said.

After a few more questions, the Court seemed satisfied with Cece's answers, although Elsmed still kept looking at her with a deep, knowing glance that she carefully avoided.

"Secrets have a way of being discovered, Ms. Amundson. Keep that in mind," he said.

The Court allowed her to leave, reminding her to let them know of anything that seemed even remotely suspicious.

"Just tell Sheriff Kasun, and he'll let us know if we need to be aware of anything," Saundra Beaumont said, and then she was dismissed.

Cece left the building in a hurry, shivering with the effort of maintaining her composure for that long. Their questions left her wondering if there might have been something to be worried about, but then she shook her head and thought there couldn't have been.

"Gregoire is dead. I sent him back to the Hell he came from. Those demons have nothing to do with me, or with him," Cece whispered. She wrapped her arms around her body and squeezed hard to keep centered. Her back itched, but she ignored it.

"I need to fly," she said out loud, even though she knew that wasn't happening tonight. She looked up at the clear night sky, marveling at the beauty of its velvety blackness sprinkled with silver stars. The moon was a bright silver color tonight, its craters visible as dove-gray splotches on its surface.

The color reminded her of the wings in her dream, and the dream reminded her of Brett. Brett, with his sad eyes and killer body, was all she could think of as she neared her store.

"Hey, you okay?"

Cece whirled around to face the object of her recent thoughts, as if she'd conjured him out of thin air. Brett. He stood up from the small bench nearby, as if he'd been waiting for her. He held out a paper cup for her.

"Sorry," he said apologetically, "it's a little cold. You were gone quite a while."

"Didn't you go back up to your cabin?" Cece asked him. She took the cup and sipped, marveling that the coffee was still lukewarm.

"We could go warm that up in your microwave," Brett said suggestively, ignoring her question.

Cece smiled, hesitated, and then turned to slip her key into the lock, and the two went through the store and up the stairs to her apartment.

Once inside, he said to her with a huskiness that sent chills up her spine, "I've been wanting to do this since I met you."

Angel or not, she needed this closeness.

When they separated, she looked into his eyes with regret, and he stiffened, aware of what she was going to say.

"I am so sorry, Brett. You are very sexy . . ."

"I know how this goes," he said bitterly, walking away from her to lean against the kitchen counter, his back to her. "You are the problem, not me . . . or how about the classic, 'I would, but . . .' fill in the blank—I am gay or I am not ready . . . Am I getting close? Is that how it is? I am sorry, but those cheesy lines are for movies or books, not real life."

His voice sounded angry and bitter, and she rushed to his side and pulled him around to face her. Cupping his face in her hands, she kissed him on the lips with all the passion she could, feeling him respond to her touch with a passion of his own that took her breath away.

"I don't understand," he said, stepping back. Holding her gently by the upper arms, he stared into her eyes. "You turn me down, and then kiss me like that? Your signals are confusing me, woman," he growled as he pulled her close once more.

She put a hand over his mouth, her eyes meeting his with a plea she hoped he could see, but knew he wouldn't.

"That's the problem," she told him with a wry smile. "I'm not the woman you think I am."

With that, she stepped out of his embrace, shivering at the sudden coldness she felt inside at the loss of his body wrapped around hers. She pointed toward the door.

"Tomorrow the camp starts. You need to get some rest, and all your equipment and clothes are at the cabin. Glenn will be there pretty early to get you, so let me see about getting you a ride."

Brett shrugged. "Don't bother. I'll walk."

He left, not giving her a chance to argue with him, and Cece watched him go, wishing she could tell him the truth. But laying on him the burden of knowing who and what she really was wouldn't help her heal him.

Sex with him, as wonderful as she knew it would be, would only complicate her goal of helping him heal the darkness that covered his heart. He already felt lost without his mother, his band, and now her, when and if he ever learned the truth.

Are you sure you want to let him go? the voice whispered in her mind.

NOTHING BUT TIME

(PINK MELON: ONE TIME MORE)

Written and sung by Brett Rhys-Falwyck

Minutes to hours to days
We got nothing but time, babe
Holding on like we have a tomorrow
when every minute testifies to our sorrow

Seconds feel like weeks as I wait
until I hold you in my arms again
We got nothing but time
until I am yours, and you are mine

Nothing but time to keep us together
Hanging on through stormy weather
Always you are my love
until we journey above

CHAPTER 17

*C*ece walked into the store just as Glenn and Brett arrived. Brett was carrying his guitar case and a larger bag, which he set down next to the counter. Turning to Cece, he kept his eyes from meeting hers, his disappointment from her rejection last night evident in the tilt of his shoulders and the way he turned from her whenever she approached him.

Following his lead, she walked toward the back of the store and pointed to the tables on which she'd put fresh blueberry scones, their scent rising and wrapping around them like a warm blueberry hug.

"Scones!" Glenn said with glee, reaching for one.

Cece slapped his hand playfully and said, as she looked over at the clock behind the counter in the front of the store, "Please wait until the others get here. Would you mind retrieving the notebooks and pens from the counter next to the cash register? I forgot to grab them on my way back here."

Glenn, grumbling about the blueberry scones not staying warm, did as she asked. Cece chuckled at his behavior, because the minute the door opened and Meghan walked in, all thoughts of scones obviously went out of his head.

Meghan, her wounds healing quickly, greeted Glenn with a big hug. He hugged her back and even gave Laine, who followed her in, a high five.

"There are scones," Glenn told the other two teens as they headed to the back, where Brett was still fiddling with his equipment and Cece was busy arranging the packets of sugar and the cups by the coffee machine.

The three teens each grabbed a scone, and amidst sighs and exclamations of pleasure at their freshness, the other students arrived. Zoey breezed in first, her smile wider when she saw the scones. Next came Elle, and immediately behind her, like a love-sick puppy, was Kase.

"Okay, everyone ready?" Brett said with a big smile for all of them. All six sets of eyes looked at him, and the teens opened their notebooks, ready to take notes.

"So, today we are going to work on our songs. The purpose of this workshop is to teach you the magic that a great song can bring to those who listen to it. If you have questions at any time during the workshop, just ask it. We are going to run this camp very casually. Okay?"

The teens all nodded.

Meghan raised her hand and said, "I'm not sure why I'm here. I don't really write songs."

Brett smiled at her. "With a voice like yours, it wouldn't hurt you to learn to write songs. So, let's begin, shall we? The first thing I want you to think about is something that makes you happy. I always find that if I think about things that put me at ease, writing songs is a lot easier. Write down five things that make you happy, and we will use them to craft a song."

Some of the teens went to work right away, and Cece could see words such as vacation, blueberry scones, puppies, kittens, Brett, and others on their pages. Others sat in thought for a while, before they, too, started jotting down things. Brett watched them working and joking with each other, and smiled.

Cece felt her heart lightening as the darkness receded from his eyes a little bit with each minute he spent with the kids. At one point, he looked up and saw her watching them, and he half smiled before turning his attention to the teens and answering a question.

Cece had decided to close the store during the camp. She knew it meant a loss of income for a few days, but felt the teens would be less likely to be distracted if she didn't have customers wandering around. Without customers, she had time to do those things she never got around to in the shop, such as sorting the paperwork that had been piling up lately. Engrossed in the vendor receipts, she didn't hear Brett until he was right beside her.

His breath on her cheek alerted her to his presence, and she jumped, putting a hand over her heart to still it. Turning, she found herself squeezed between his body and the back of the counter.

"Hey," she said softly, her breath betraying her nervousness at having him so close.

"The kids are hungry. Are we sending them out for lunch, or did you have something catered?"

Cece looked at the clock in surprise. Time had flown!

"There should be a couple of pizzas arriving any minute now," Cece started to say when her comment was interrupted by a knock at the door.

"Pizza!" the teens said in unison. Glenn raced to the door, grabbed the boxes, and took them to the tables. Cece chuckled as she paid the delivery person. Going upstairs to her kitchen, she got out paper plates and plastic silverware before returning downstairs. Most of the pizza was gone by the time she returned, and she shook her head in amusement, a small smile twisting her lips.

"Thanks for leaving a slice for me," she said, grabbing a

pepperoni slice she could see Kase eyeing hungrily. "Tomorrow I will make sure to order more."

"Might be a good idea," Brett said, chuckling as he pulled a slice out of the hands of Laine, who groaned and grabbed another slice.

"So, how's it going? Are you all enjoying it?"

"Yep, it's great," said Laine. "I'm learning a lot."

The other teens nodded in agreement.

"Okay, let's get back to work," Brett said. "You all have your first line, and your refrain, so now you have to decide if it will be a rhyming song, or a free verse."

Cece retreated as they returned to business. A few hours later and the teens were heading out the door.

"Tomorrow we will start on the music. Thanks, guys. You all did a great job."

Goodbyes were said, and then they were all out the door, with Glenn, Laine, and Meghan the last ones out.

Cece closed the door behind them and turned to Brett. "I forgot to ask Glenn to give you a ride back up to the cabin."

"I told him I was fine."

"You're not going to walk, are you? It's going to be dark soon, and it's pretty cold."

Cece saw the look in his eyes, and her heart suddenly started fluttering.

"I thought we could go out, have something to eat, and then maybe talk?" His eyes watched her carefully for a reaction.

Cece hesitated, knowing she should say no. Knowing she wanted to say yes.

"Yes, sure," she said without realizing the words were out of her mouth. "My jacket's upstairs. I'll be right back."

Heading up the stairs two at a time, she surprised herself with how the thought of having dinner with this gorgeous man was exciting her. She wouldn't think about the consequences of dinner and conversation; she would just enjoy it, she decided.

When she came back downstairs, Brett was standing with his back to her. She could see his face in profile, and it broke her heart to see the sadness had returned.

Slipping her arms around his waist, she rested her cheek on his back and whispered, "Why so blue, dream lover?"

"What?" Brett turned quickly, capturing her in an embrace. She lowered her face, but he brought her chin up until she looked him in the eyes. "What did you just say?"

Cece started to deny saying anything, but instead she reached up and drew his face down to hers and softly pressed her lips to his. She broke their embrace before he had a chance to tighten his hold and pointed to the door.

"Shall we go?" she said a little breathlessly.

He nodded after a moment of studying her. He did not reach for her again.

At dinner, this time at Whisper Falls Inn's dining room, she asked him how he thought things were going with the camp.

"It's going great," Brett enthused, excited to be talking about the teens and their obvious interest and talents. "They are all very good students."

"Yes, they seem to like this. So what will you do tomorrow?"

"We worked on lyrics today, so tomorrow I thought we would work on understanding the interplay between notes and lyrics and what notes set the mood. You can increase the speed of the notes so many ways, and that can be a phenomenal way to set a mood; or you can slow it way down," he said, emphasizing the last two words by drawing them out, "to set another kind of mood."

Playing with her food, Cece looked at him with a twinkle in her eye and said, "And what kind of mood would our love song have?"

Brett was obviously taken aback by her question, looking like he was about to spit out his drink. Cece rushed over to slap him on the back until he regained control of his cough.

"Sorry," she said in a tone that didn't sound like she was sorry. "I didn't mean to upset you."

"Upset me?" Brett swallowed hard to regain his breath. "You just took me by surprise."

Cece grew quiet. "You didn't answer my question."

Locking eyes, the two looked at each other with the certainty that comes from knowing they would soon be in bed together.

Brett laid his silverware down and said, "Shall we get the check?"

"Yes," Cece breathed, not taking her eyes from his.

Walking back to her apartment, neither spoke. What was there to say, after all?

As they moved into her bedroom, Brett stopped and turned her to face him. Cupping her face like she had done to his earlier, he kissed her gently, his lips barely touching hers as he gauged her reaction to his touch.

She didn't move away, and he grew bolder.

Cece, knowing this was crazy, knowing they had no future together because of what she was and what he wasn't, and knowing that this might unravel everything she was trying to do for him, let him lead her to the bed.

He laid her down and climbed into the bed next to her. Clothes and shoes practically fell off them as they learned about each other's bodies. Cece held him close, directing him to what she needed even as he helped her discover his desires. Sighs and whispers were the only music they needed as they climaxed in a symphony of pleasures they found with each other.

Afterward, they lay in bed exhausted, and Cece held him until he fell asleep.

She slipped out of bed and went to the bathroom. She leaned against the mirror over the sink, feeling overwhelmed. Even with all her good intentions, she'd still managed to fall into bed with him without considering the consequences. She had been able to keep herself under control this time, but what about next time? She couldn't let this happen again.

Was it as good as it was with us?

The voice intruded in her thoughts and was gone before she could fully comprehend what had just happened.

SHE HELD HIS HAND, *her fingers small inside his larger one.*

They were going to fly.

They were at the edge of the cliff.

He turned to her, smiling, his grip tightening on her hand as darkness clouded his eyes.

He couldn't see her anymore.

Her hand stayed in his, but her body disappeared into the inky blackness.

He called out to her, his voice harsh and angry to his ears.

Twisting this way and that, he searched for her.

Then there was a white light, a beautiful white light, and in the center of it she stood.

Her wings were singed, their white cooled to a light gray, as if she were ill.

He tried to touch her, but she ran from him, ran toward the cliff as if to take flight.

She was trying to fly away, but he couldn't let her do that. She was his.

He couldn't let her go, couldn't let her leave.

Just as he reached her, she tried to fly, panic and fear in her eyes.

He laughed, but it wasn't his laugh. It was something darker, something evil.

Reaching out, he grabbed her just as she took to the air.

They both fell, his weight too much for her fragile wings, and they tore from her body, hanging by just a single feather.

He laughed as they fell, spiraling out of control.

She turned in his arms and held his face, whispering in his ears even as air rushed past them.

"Wake up, darling, wake up. It's just a dream."

"Wake up, Brett. Darling. Wake up."

Brett stirred, and Cece relaxed. For a minute there, she didn't think he would come out of the dream at all. He had been in so deep. She clapped her hand to her chest, feeling the cross pendant under it as she tried to still her heart, and hoping he wouldn't notice the panic in her eyes.

This dream had been so much darker.

Looking in his face, she searched his eyes to see if he still bore traces of that darkness, certain she saw something in his eyes that was wrong, but then it was gone.

"Sorry," he said. "I keep having these weird dreams." He was shaking.

Cece nodded at his explanation. "It's time to get up anyway. Do you want to take a shower?"

"Join me?" he said with a lascivious grin that made her laugh at him. Slapping him playfully on his bare shoulder, she shook her head.

"No time. The kids will be here soon. I'll meet you downstairs."

Glenn and Meghan were standing outside the store waiting for her when she got there. Unlocking the door, she let the teens inside. They immediately headed back to the tables, followed by the other teens, who came in within minutes of Glenn.

Laine was the last to arrive, and he was acting a little more than suspicious. He nodded to Meghan, whose face lit up before she masked her expression at a glance from Glenn.

Well, that was interesting, Cece thought, observing the way Laine and Meghan kept grinning and giggling, only stopping at puzzled looks from Glenn or one of the other teens.

Brett helped each of the teens with time in the recording studio to work on the music for their individual songs. Everyone seemed to really enjoy themselves, judging by the laughter and jokes that passed between all of them.

Cece put the paper plates on the tables at lunchtime as their meal arrived. The teens were all talking at once, poking and pushing each other playfully, except for Meghan and Laine, who had slipped away and were talking with Brett intently.

He listened with that *totally into you* way he had—his head tilted slightly, his eyes locked on whoever was speaking, his body relaxed and leaning toward the speaker. It made her feel like she was the only one in his world when he did that to her, so she was sure the teens were feeling the same.

It was a special talent to be able to command the attention of so many young people with so many interests, and yet he handled it all with such grace and fun. He was a natural leader, Cece realized. And part of that was his sincerity and genuine desire to help. His generosity oozed out of him.

He is special, isn't he? More special than you realize, but you'll know just how special very soon. Very soon. Very soon.

Cece frowned. The voice was insistent and irresistible. She looked up just as Brett met her gaze. He looked worried, but she waved him off. She was fine, her gesture said, and he returned to the teens, who were asking a lot of questions today.

As they filed out, their hands drumming beats on each other's shoulders and their notebooks, the teens called out a thank you and left.

The minute the door closed behind them and silence reigned again, Cece realized just how potent silence could be.

"Day two under the belt," Brett said with an exhausted sigh. "I never realized how much work something like this could be. Those teens never stopped asking questions. But . . . I wouldn't trade it for anything. This has been fun."

Cece smiled. "You're a natural at this. I'm surprised you've never done anything like this before."

Brett chuckled. "I think until this very moment, I never realized I could do this, but it is something I would like to do again."

He looked at her with an intensity that led Cece to believe he wasn't just talking about the camp.

She smiled as he suggested they lock things up and head back upstairs.

"My ride's gone," he said, his gaze not leaving her face. He reached out and touched her cheek, his finger sliding down to trace her jawline before he leaned in for a kiss.

She didn't say no.

DAY THREE FOUND the teens excitedly comparing lyrics and songs. Meghan, bless her, was a willing participant in the singing part of the practices, as she was going to sing pretty much everyone's song if they weren't singing themselves. Cece had to admit the shy girl had a beautiful voice.

She and Brett were both so exhausted when the day ended that they fell into bed, sleeping the whole night through without any more disturbing dreams, for which she was grateful. That last one had taken a lot out of her.

Brett seemed so much happier, and she had hopes that she was going to be able to help him. Looking at him sleeping next to her, she sighed with contentment. His arm lying across her chest was both comforting and solid.

She traced the dragon tattoo on his back with her finger, marveling at the intricacy of the design. *His ability to withstand pain must be high*, she thought, remembering how her ankle had burned for days when she'd had her small tattoo done. He'd told her he thought her halo was perfect because she was "his angel," and he would have picked that exact tattoo if it had been up to him.

Snuggling next to him, his breath tickling her shoulder, she sighed, thinking she'd never been so happy. He stirred, and leaning into her, he kissed her, pulling her on top of him and sighing with happiness when they were done.

"I'll love you forever," he said, touching her nose with the tip of his finger.

"Same," she said with a large smile. He traced her lips with his finger before leaning in for a kiss that took her breath away. Then, with a big yawn, he settled back in and pulled her closer.

She was so happy, she ignored the voice that whispered to her as she fell into sleep. *Enjoy your sleep now, my beautiful bird, for soon you will sleep no more.*

CATCHING THE DREAM

(PINK MELON: ONE TIME MORE)

Written and sung by Brett Rhys-Falwyck

Before the dreamers
there were the hopers
Before the hopers
there were the hopeless

When the dream becomes the thing that holds you back
you gotta dust yourself off and get rid of the slack
Nothing should come between
the hopers and the dream

Take the dream to the next level
Pull up them socks and hustle
Get out and make things go
before you are six feet below

When the dream becomes the thing that holds you back
you gotta dust yourself off and get rid of the slack
Nothing should come between
the hopers and the dream

Into the void of what you don't know
That is where all lost dreams go
Jump in with both feet
Never accept defeat

When the dream becomes the thing that holds you back
you gotta dust yourself off and get rid of the slack
Nothing should come between
the hopers and the dream

If you fail, if you lose, if you make no change
nothing's lost, you just take the dream and rearrange
Hold your heart out for all to see
The dream will keep its purity

When the dream becomes the thing that holds you back
you gotta dust yourself off and get rid of the slack
Nothing should come between
the hopers and the dream

CHAPTER 18

*D*ay four dawned, and the teens' excitement jumped forward exponentially. Tonight was the concert.

They had a few hours to practice their songs, and then they were to break so they could go home and change into their clothes for the performance.

After gathering their things, the teens left, still talking animatedly with Brett, except for Laine and Meghan, who asked if they could have one more time in the studio.

"Why?" Cece said, looking at them with a puzzled expression. "Didn't you get enough time to practice already?"

"This isn't our song for the show, well, not exactly," Meghan stammered.

Cece looked at her and said, "Meghan, what are you and Laine up to?"

Looking to Laine for permission, which he gave with a nod of his head, she said with a huge grin, "Today is Glenn's birthday, and we're going to sing a song I wrote for him. Don't tell him, okay?"

"So that's what the two of you were working on all those times you were in the studio together." Cece slapped her forehead to emphasize how stupid she was. "I should have realized that."

"So can we?"

"Yes, Meghan, this is a wonderful idea. He'll love it."

Meghan and Laine scrambled into the studio and began to play their song. Glenn walked back in just as they finished and saw Meghan hug Laine. The look on his face immediately grew dark and angry. Before Cece could catch him, he ran back out and down the street. By the time she got around the counter and out the door, he was driving away, too fast for her to catch him.

Calling him, she wasn't surprised when it went to voicemail. She asked him to call her. Not sure if she should spoil Meghan's surprise or not, she didn't tell him the reason why he needed to call her.

Brett came back in just as Meghan and Laine left. Without a word to Cece, he went upstairs. She watched him go, surprised at how stiff he was walking and wondering why.

She followed him upstairs and dressed quickly. He kissed her gently, his eyes promising so much more later that night.

"I'll meet you at the Annex, got an errand to run first. See you there." Then he was downstairs and out of the shop before she could catch her breath.

The silence descended over her like a shroud, and Cece shivered, feeling something dark moving in that silence.

GREG GRANITE SMILED, but the smile didn't reach his eyes. It barely reached his lips, but inside, he was grinning.

Amanda shivered. Her compulsion to do as he bid her was wasting her away. Like her two companions, she was unable to shake the spell woven by Greg Granite that had forced her to sleep with the rock star and forge his signature on the documents that now lay before them on the table.

In his hand, Greg Granite held a knife, the same knife he'd been holding to her throat for the last half hour. Every time he laughed, he let the knife slip just a little on her skin, then he would lick the knife and smack his lips like he was eating a fine meal.

She could feel the blood running down her throat to pool just below the collar of her pristine white shirt, slowly staining it crimson.

"Won't be long now, my beauty, before this is all over."

Amanda wasn't sure if he meant her, or this mysterious woman he called Cecelia.

Amanda glanced out the corner of her eye at her two friends, Mark and Joe, both of whom bore equal marks on their necks, with blood slowly coagulating on their wounds. They met her gaze with wide eyes, and in them, she saw the same fear she felt. What was happening? How did things get this way?

Greg Granite had come to Forthright a few months ago with an influx of cash and a very persuasive argument, and talked himself into a partnership with their elderly owner, Graham Chadwick. Upon Mr. Chadwick's unexpected death from a heart attack, Greg had taken ownership of the company, and that's when things started to go bad.

At first, Amanda had found his attention flattering, and then it became weird really quickly. Dinners where she would go home with no memory of anything after the main course and find bruises all over her body. Wine that tasted like blood, and strange conversations she would overhear between Mr. Granite and someone else, someone he only referred to as "Mr. X." And then there was the campaign to ruin Pink Melon and capture Brett Rhys-Falwyck in an unbreakable contract.

"Do you understand what is about to happen?" he asked her

with a smile. A gleeful smile, she thought. One that made her shiver with relief that she wasn't the one he was after.

Amanda shook her head, trying not to whimper as he brought the knife closer to her throat once more. He leaned in, his sulfur-scented breath nearly making her gag and throw up her lunch, but she held onto herself, just barely.

"Oh, of course you don't. How could you? You aren't like us." He said nothing else, just continued to cackle and carve her neck like she was a prize steak he wanted to savor. And savor he did. Her blood seemed to be the main course on his menu.

WHEN CECE ARRIVED at the Annex, she was pleased to see it was crowded with teens, parents, and other members of the community. She nodded to several people she knew as she made her way backstage to where all the teens were waiting to take their turns on stage.

Glenn wasn't there.

"Okay, everyone, gather here," Brett said. He gestured for the group to stand near him. They complied, nervous giggles and shifting feet sure signs of the butterflies in their stomachs. Cece couldn't blame them.

"Where's Glenn?" Brett called out.

"Here," Glenn said from the background.

Cece made her way over to him, but when she gestured for him to join the rest, he shook his head in refusal and turned his back to her, as if checking on the audience.

Cece reached out and touched him on the shoulder, but he shrugged her off. "Glenn, I have something to tell you, something you might like to know."

Glenn opened his mouth to say something, but closed it again when Brett stepped out on the stage and addressed the audience.

"Hello, everyone. Thank you for being here tonight to support these very talented teens. First, I would like to thank a few people for their assistance with the camp." Brett read from a list of names on his paperwork. "Without further ado, I would like to bring out our first duo to perform their original song, 'Special Day,' written and sung by Meghan Gonzalez, with Laine Greenhill on the guitar."

Brett clapped, encouraging the audience to follow suit.

Glenn snorted and started to turn away when Meghan spoke into the microphone.

"Hello, everyone. I am super excited to be here because tonight is the very special day of a very special friend of mine. I wrote this song with Laine to wish a happy birthday to Glenn Johnson, everyone. Come on out here, Glenn."

Glenn looked sheepishly at Cece, his cheeks flooding with color. She smiled and pushed him onto the stage.

Meghan pulled a stool over and asked him to sit. With a nod to Laine, she sang her song to him, promising to love him forever. Glenn couldn't take his eyes off her.

At the end of the song, while the audience applauded and whistled, he pulled Meghan into his arms and kissed her.

Brett stepped up to the microphone after first whispering something to Meghan and Glenn that caused them both to blush. They were still blushing as they left the stage.

Glenn looked at Cece as he passed her and stopped. Meghan stopped, too. Her grip on Glenn's hand tightened, as if she was afraid to let him go.

"Meghan, don't you have to sing with Elle on the next song?" Cece asked.

"Oh yeah, guess I'd better go." She kissed Glenn on the lips before returning to the stage.

As each teen took the stage in turn, Cece was impressed by their songs and their talents. So much talent.

Brett joined in on guitar with each of the solos, and when it came to the last performance, each of the students came back on stage to lend their guitar or their voice to the finale.

Cece, face shining with happiness, couldn't stop clapping.

As the final note rang out, Brett pointed to each of the teens who took a bow and then they pointed to Brett for more applause.

Brett, blushing, waved his hands for everyone to stop, and the audience became silent.

Without a microphone, Brett started to speak. "Thank you. There's a pretty talented group of folks on this stage, isn't there?"

A few shouts came from the audience that caused some chuckles and a smattering of claps, and Brett waved everyone to silence again. He'd slung his guitar back over his chest and strummed a few chords while he spoke.

He talked about how much he loved his visit to Havenwood Falls, about how his troubles back home had made this trip seem like a wonderful chance to start fresh, about how he'd been duped into signing a contract he didn't remember signing, and how that had caused people to think he'd abandoned them. He talked about his mother's passing and how hard that had been on him and how he'd started drinking to get over the pain.

"But since arriving here in Havenwood Falls, I haven't had a drop of alcohol, and I don't miss it. I owe it all to the teens who participated in the first Havenwood Falls Music Camp, and to Cece Amundson, owner of Havenwood Falls Music & More and organizer of this whole thing. Cece, will you come out here and take a bow?"

Cece, surprised and a bit embarrassed, wasn't sure she should come out, but when Glenn and Meghan, sensing her reluctance, grabbed her by her arms and pulled her out, she smiled graciously and blew a kiss to the audience.

"Now, Cece, take a seat here." Brett pulled one of the stools up next to her and then a second one, on which he sat. The teens stood around them with big smiles on their faces, and Cece wasn't sure what to do, so she folded her hands in her lap and waited to see what was going to happen next.

Next involved flowers and a gift from the teens that turned out to be a small gold bracelet.

"I'd like to share with you my own song from the class. Kids, ready?"

They nodded, and Brett began to strum his guitar, his eyes locked onto hers as if he was only singing to her.

Rock me gently in your arms
Only your love can keep me from harm
I never knew peace until I found you
Without your love I don't know what I'll do
I need your touch like the sun needs the moon
like oceans need the shore, and a fork needs a spoon
like the stars need the night
like the dark needs the light
your heart beating next to mine is all I need
So rock me gently, let's plant the seed
Be my darling forever
my angel of never

OVERCOME by emotion as she listened to him sing and pour his heart out to her, Cece nearly broke down. She didn't know what to say. How could she promise him forever? Her kind couldn't marry a human, couldn't bear children, and he deserved so much more.

Without realizing what she was doing, Cece jumped off the stool and ran off the stage. Ignoring the gasps from the audience and running from the building, she raced toward the mountain, her only thought to get someplace where she could spread her wings and fly. Fly away from all the hurt she knew she was about to cause to someone she'd just wanted to help.

Reaching her launching point, she unzipped her dress and slipped out of it. In her slip and shoes, she twitched her shoulders and was about to jump off to take flight when she was jerked back into the hardness of a chest.

"It's you. You're the woman in my dreams. How is this possible? What are you? Who are you?"

Cece turned in Brett's arms, an incredulous expression on his face. She could hear shouts down the trail, but ignored them as Brett's mouth twitched and his body shivered in the chilly night air. Her wings were flapping with the need to fly, but she ignored them too.

Something was happening to Brett. Before her eyes, he was changing, morphing, a darkness spreading over his face. Smoke poured from his eyes, materializing to stand next to her as Brett collapsed at her feet.

"Hello, Gregoire," Cece said in resignation.

"Hello, my darling Cecelia," the demon said as he gave her the once-over. He was gray, and tall, and slender. His face shifted from demon gray to human pale as he reasserted his own form. His arms and legs were covered with a smoky haze that imitated clothing. He circled her as he studied her, his dark eyes trapping her as effectively as a vise.

Her wings continued to flutter, but she was unable to move her feet. The demon had cemented ice around her feet, and she was his prisoner. Taking a deep breath, she smiled even though she was breaking inside. "What do you want, Gregoire?"

"You know what I want, angel," he hissed as he moved closer to her. "You know very well what you took from me."

Cece paled, but covered her fear by laughing at him.

"Surely you know about the wards here at Havenwood Falls. How could I have traveled here with it?"

"The games end now," Gregoire said as he pointed to Brett's unconscious form. "Or do you really love your lover so little that you will sacrifice his life for your desire for a bauble that doesn't belong to you?"

Brett twitched, his body reacting involuntarily to the pain of whatever torture Gregoire was perpetrating.

"Humans are so frail, aren't they?" Gregoire sent another bolt of magic into Brett to make his point.

Cece cried out, a growl more than a sob, which made Gregoire laugh again as he poked at the body of the unconscious rock star with his magic.

In an effort to distract him, Cece said calmly, "I will get it for you, but first, you need to free me."

"How stupid do you think I am, angel?" he hissed as he moved closer to her.

Cece's wings fluttered faster the closer he came. Cece ignored them. She needed to focus on Gregoire. She needed to distract him. She'd seen Brett's eyes flutter open, seen him assess the situation.

If she could get Gregoire to come close enough, she could fly away with him and save Brett.

But Gregoire was no fool, and he stopped just out of reach.

"I need that, Cecelia. If you don't hand it over now, nothing will save you from the fate I have planned for you. And darling," he purred, "you don't want that to happen, now do you? You know what I'm capable of."

Cece knew he was serious. Gregoire never lied, never bluffed. He didn't need to. He had all the power of darkness behind him. But then, she had the power of light behind her. If she could only get him a little closer, she might have a chance to defeat him . . . again.

She could hear people on the trail below them. She had to keep talking and distract Gregoire so he wouldn't notice them. At least if she died, Brett would live, and then her sacrifice would be worth it.

"Gregoire, I need to get my hands free. Release me."

"Oh no, I don't think so."

"You have Brett. You can use him to keep me in line. I won't try anything while he's still here."

Gregoire searched her eyes and seemed to believe her. She felt the spell holding her in place loosen enough.

Lunging forward, she grabbed for him, but he anticipated the move and slipped out of her grip. Her wings stilled as she realized he had turned with murderous intent in his eyes to Brett, who was just coming to full consciousness.

"Stop! Here, take it! Just leave him alone." Cece began to remove the cross necklace from around her neck.

The demon had taken her true love the last time they fought over the pendant. She wouldn't let that happen to Brett, too. She wasn't sure Gregoire could even use the vessel—it was made to capture souls, but for the Divine, not for Hell—yet he coveted it nonetheless. It must have had some kind of value, for him to follow her here. Last time, she didn't want to chance letting him have it— and she'd paid for that decision dearly. With her love's life. With her own heart. She wouldn't make that mistake again.

"Glad to see you've finally come to your senses," Gregoire said with glee. He nearly danced over to her, reaching to pull the necklace from her as she fiddled with the clasp. Instead, she grabbed his hand at the same time Brett rushed them both and Elsmed Fairchild entered the clearing.

Speaking three words, "*Eum ad infernum,*" the fae pointed to Gregoire, who screamed once and turned into smoke before disappearing.

Elsmed looked at Cece with a sad expression, but at least it was an improvement over his usual one.

"You know we'll have to discuss this" was all he said before leaving the clearing with several other members of the Court of the Sun and the Moon, none of whom spoke to her.

Brett looked at her with eyes full of confusion. "Who are you? Where am I?" Gripping his head, he whispered, "What's going on here? Why do I feel so . . . light? So free?"

"You're welcome," Elsmed said over his shoulder as he walked back down the mountain.

She understood. Not only did he take care of Gregoire, but he also took care of Brett—ensuring that the human out-of-towner would remember nothing about this. Nothing about her.

Swallowing down her sadness, Cece looked at Brett with a small smile and simply said, "Lovely night for a stroll in the moonlight, isn't it?"

HUNDREDS OF MILES AWAY, Amanda, trapped inside her mind as the pain escalated, prayed for release.

Perhaps it was the prayers, or perhaps it was the night crew, but somehow Amanda felt the compulsion lifting as Greg was distracted by the African American janitor, with the name Brad on his shirt, who insisted he had to clean the room. Whatever the cause, Greg was suddenly gone, and the janitor was handing them all clean, white towels. On the desk, the contracts Greg had been so gleefully exalting over disappeared, too.

Brad told the men they had not been here tonight and that they'd merely cut themselves shaving. To Amanda, he said she had accidentally burned herself while straightening her hair. They didn't argue. They took their towels, rushed to the elevator, and somehow found themselves home.

The next day, Amanda came back to the office to find an email from Mr. Granite stating he'd retired and that there had been a fire in the file room and several contracts had been lost.

Amanda was happy to discover the ones for Brett Rhys-Falwyck and Pink Melon had been among those lost, and since Greg hadn't bothered to file them in the computer electronically, they were gone forever.

~

BRETT'S abrupt departure from Havenwood Falls didn't go unnoticed, but Cece explained it away as his needing to return home for an emergency court date.

Back in the store a few days later, she was packing away the new shipment of CDs when Meghan and Glenn walked in hand in hand. Each carried a coffee. They couldn't stop looking at each other. Behind them, Laine walked in, holding a coffee for her.

"Thank you, Laine." She held out her hand to accept the coffee.

"Did you hear?" Glenn asked her when he saw the CDs.

"Hear what?" Cece asked without knowing what Glenn could possibly referring to.

"The band is hoping to get back together. Pink Melon."

"Oh?"

"Yeah, that's what I saw on the internet. I think they have some legal stuff to work out, but they hope to start a new tour soon."

"Really? That's awesome," Cece said, and she meant it. She could feel the weight lifting off Brett and felt glad she had helped some small measure in his new happiness. Her heart skipped a beat at the memory of him, and she turned to wipe away a tear. Accepting his departure had been the hardest part of this whole encounter, but she knew he would be so much happier with his new life.

And yet, that thought was small consolation.

"Goodbye, love. You are the true fly away angel. The angel of my heart."

EPILOGUE

$\mathcal{A}$manda straightened her skirt and knocked on the door. Not sure what kind of reception she would get, she stepped back slightly. She touched the side of her neck, where the strange scars had all but disappeared. Her life had been spiraling out of control ever since she'd met this rocker, and she needed to set things right. Coming here was the first step to regaining control of her life.

Brett opened the door. He was wearing a pair of sweatpants and nothing else. Both his chest and feet were bare, and Amanda swallowed hard as she tried not to stare at his perfectly muscled abs.

But it was nearly impossible not to stare at his luscious lips.

"What do you want?" he asked wearily, as if talking were a great effort.

"I . . . I came to apologize," Amanda said, swallowing hard. She wasn't sure where to start. How could she explain all the craziness that had been her life in the last few months? And how could she apologize to this man when the words were stuck in her throat?

She saw his eyes travel to her throat and then look away. She saw a small flush creep across his cheeks as if he was embarrassed she caught him looking.

"I guess you can come in." Brett said this as he walked away. He grabbed a bottle of water from the island in the kitchen and continued walking onto the back deck.

She followed, slipping her shoes off as she did so. If he was going to be barefoot, then so was she.

He gestured for her to take a chair nearby, and he sat so that he faced the ocean at the end of his private beach. She wondered, not for the first time, what it would be like to be this rich. Would she appreciate it?

"You have a beautiful view," she said to him, trying to keep the envy out of her voice.

"Yeah," he said, "thanks." He took a swig of the water and then glanced at her.

Now it was her turn to blush, and she tried not to let him see it, lowering her head and hiding her face in her curtain of hair, suddenly self-conscious.

"Don't do that," Brett said gently, reaching out to brush her hair off her face and over her shoulder.

"I'm so sorry," she whispered to him, her eyes large and sincere.

"I know," he said in a whisper. "Everyone's sorry."

She bit her lip, not sure how to answer that, and then remembered why she was there.

"I have a story to tell you," she said quietly, touching him on the arm to get his attention.

When she finished, he stared at her without speaking.

"You believe me, don't you?"

"Yes, I do, but you probably shouldn't tell anyone else." He leaned forward, his hands warm on her arms. "You were part of something you can never understand, and not something I can explain to you. Something that goes far beyond good, or evil, or rock stars."

His lips twitched into a wry smile as he said this. Amanda opened her mouth to speak, but he put a finger over her lips, a finger that slowly traveled down her throat to touch her scars.

"These," he whispered, "are nothing to be ashamed of. You survived a battle you didn't even know you were part of. A battle that has been going on a long time. You are a survivor, and so am I. The world will rock on gently, with or without us, but it will never be the same world."

"I think you have your own story to tell," Amanda said, looking deeply into his eyes.

"And someday I will tell you about it," he said softly. "But today is not made for sadness or stories about loss. It is a day for a walk on the beach, and burying our feet in the sand and surf."

He stood up. Holding out his hand, he said to her, "Walk with me?"

"Forever," she said, without understanding why those words were so perfect for this moment, but happy to know, when she saw his grin light up his eyes, that they were enough to bring him peace.

FLY AWAY ANGEL

(BRETT RHYS-FALWYCK SOLO ALBUM: OCEANS)

Written and sung by Brett Rhys-Falwyck

I saw you fall from far away
I raced to help, but you left anyway
Bereft, I stand where you once stood
Your muse my purpose, I understood

Fly away angel
on winds of promise
Fly away angel
Nothing else can be, but this

I held the feathers of our lost dreams
floating like petals on an alabaster scene
Nothing but air to hold you aloft
Enough, enough, I say, wind-tossed

Fly away angel
on winds of promise
Fly away angel
Nothing else can be, but this

I spread my wings and fly
to join you in the skies
Our hopes, our dreams, our need to be
overwhelming the senses that color me

Fly away angel
on winds of promise
Fly away angel
Nothing else can be, but this

No more ghosts to fear
Just you, held gently near
Never to fly, never to leave
My heart is full, and I believe

Fly away angel
You hold fast to me
Fly away angel
I will never leave

We hope you enjoyed this story in the Havenwood Falls series
featuring a variety of supernatural creatures. The series is a
collaborative effort by multiple authors.

Havenwood Falls books by Susan Burdorf:

Old Wounds by Susan Burdorf
Rock Me Gently by Susan Burdorf

Also look for the YA line, Havenwood Falls High; the historical paranormal line, Legends of Havenwood Falls; the sexier side of town, Havenwood Falls Sin & Silk; the local supernatural college, Sun & Moon Academy; and the Havenwood Falls holiday short story anthologies.

Stay up to date at www.HavenwoodFalls.com

ABOUT THE AUTHOR

Susan Burdorf is an avid reader, photographer, and lover of all things sparkly. Writing is a passion that is only quenched when THE END is written on the last page of a manuscript. Nothing says home to her, though, like the presence of her family. Susan encourages you to correspond with her and is available for public appearances at schools and conferences. You can reach her through her social media contacts listed below.

Facebook: www.facebook.com/susanburdorfauthor
Twitter and Instagram: @sburdorf

ACKNOWLEDGMENTS

Thank you to all the Havenwood Falls High authors who allowed me to borrow their characters for my story; to Kallie Ross Mathews, Amy Hale, and Kristie Cook—who is one of the most amazing people I know. Also, a huge thank you to Liz Ferry for the hard work keeping us in line (so many books, so little time, but you are crazy good at what you do!). Regina Wamba, you are the artist of all things covers. Thank you for making my words look good between the covers. Thank you to my readers, who let me take them on this wild ride and offer suggestions and praise where needed. Know that without you, I would not enjoy what I do half as much as I do.

A Havenwood Falls New Adult Novella

HAVENWOOD FALLS

FROM THE EMBERS

AMY MILES

From the Embers (A Havenwood Falls Novella) by Amy Miles

Nineteen-year-old Ember Ramsey creates trouble everywhere she goes, and right now, she's on the warpath. Driven to avenge her momma's brutal murder, she infiltrates a world of bloodthirsty monsters, but as a flame-wielding fighter, she might be the deadliest of them all. When she enters a fight club in Denver to squeeze information out of a known snitch, she comes face to face with the black-eyed demon who haunts her nightmares.

With her mark finally in sight, Ember trails the killer to a quaint mountain town. But when her welcoming committee includes a nosy rent-a-cop, a cocky local with suspicious connections, and a whole slew of supernaturals living side by side, Ember realizes that Havenwood Falls is no ordinary town. Finding her momma's killer just got a whole lot harder.

Never before has Ember been so close to her goal, but with each step she takes, her control weakens. Soon the fires will spread, and Ember is no longer sure she can hold back the incredible power she possesses. Or that she wants to—even if it means burning Havenwood Falls to the ground.

FROM THE EMBERS

AN EXCERPT

Smart people knew to duck when the world took a swing at them. I guess I hadn't learned that lesson yet. Taking a hit was something I knew how to do. Knowing when to stop before my luck ran out—well, that was another story.

A cheer rose from the crowd. My hair blocked the view of the approaching wall, but I sure felt it. With a groan, I collapsed into the gutter. The murky water tasted of rotting trash, and I didn't want to think of what else. I spit to the side before I rolled to my back.

That one hurt.

"You sure you're up for another round, Ember?" Two glowing orb-like eyes stared down at me. They looked far too small compared to the eggplant-sized nose they flanked. "You're lookin' a bit rough after Fluffy took that last chunk out of you."

The troll wasn't wrong.

A single tear rolled down my cheek, and I caught it with my fingertip. It shimmered there like a summer sunset against the night. The instant I touched it to the gouge in my right side, sweet relief rushed in. Having healing powers sure came in handy.

"Whoever named that seven-foot-tall bastard of a skinwalker Fluffy deserves to have their head kicked in," I said.

I'd been fighting against scum like him for six years, but he was my first skinwalker. The stories were few and far between. Some relayed tales of creatures that could assume the skin of a man instead of a beast. Staring up at Fluffy's three heads, I wished I'd taken on one of them instead.

Fuzzbert laughed. "That's my girl."

The hand that yanked me to my feet was the size of a large serving platter, dotted with tufts of hair. It was a tight squeeze to escape around his belly. The friction of his wet poncho trapped me. I wiggled free and leaned against the wall to catch my breath.

There were dozens of wounds in need of healing, but they would have to wait. Fluffy paced, watching me. Saliva dripped in thick strings from his gaping jaws. Blood matted the soaked fur near one of his right eyes and his hind leg. It was hard to tell which of his three heads was the dominant one. They were all glaring at me with blackened hatred through the rain.

Fluffy made the hound of Hades look like a puppy. Not exactly fair in hand-to-hand combat, but most street-fighting clubs didn't have rules. At least not rules that went in favor of anyone but the man in charge. Or rather the troll in charge, in this case.

Like most in the crowd, Fuzzbert waited for me to call the fight. Like heck was I tapping out. A lot of money was riding on this.

But I wasn't here for the money.

"Ember?" Fuzzbert stepped toward me. He cast a wary glance at the sky. Trolls didn't like lightning.

I held up my hand. "I need a minute to breathe."

That last hit was the hardest I'd ever taken. Fluffy must have been on steroids. Or a drug that was less than legal.

I'd fared well enough against two of his heads, but that third one literally bit me in the backside. It was a shame they confiscated my dagger at the start of the fight. I'd love to stake one of his heads to the wall.

"Time's up, Ember." The crowd pressed in closer to hear Fuzzbert. They were a rainbow of colors, each with ponchos of various sizes. Folks in Denver sure took their fight clubs seriously. "Are you tapping out?"

Wiping a mixture of blood and rain from my brow, I grinned and thumped Fuzzbert on his warty nose.

"If you were half as smart as you are ugly, you'd already know the answer to that."

Fuzzbert's breath wheezed around the gap in his lips. Crooked teeth, as long as my fingers, jutted from his gums.

"Speak for yourself." His laugh sounded like an old lady who'd smoked for three lifetimes.

"Aw, come on, Fuzz. You know it's not nice to make a girl cry," I said.

I wasn't as ugly as a troll, but I wasn't a beauty queen either, thanks to a run-in I had a few years ago with fire. Turns out healing tears did squat on that.

Fluffy's hackles rose at the first rumble of thunder in the distance. He squared off with me. A sharp bark sent the crowd back to clear the area.

"That mutt has got a hair up his backside tonight." Fuzzbert might look menacing to most, but I knew his sweet spot. He loved money. It didn't matter how he got it.

I palmed him the last bit of cash I had to my name. "I need some information. He's going to give it up, one way or another."

The troll shook his head. "It's your funeral."

"You'd better be careful, Fuzz." I tied my hair back into a semblance of a bun. "Someone might think you've gone soft on a human."

He snorted and stomped away. If I wasn't paying so well, he'd probably eat me for that comment.

"Hurry up. Place your bets." Fuzzbert cast a scowl at the clouds. "I haven't got all night."

I leaned against the wall, trying to appear unconcerned as Fluffy paced. There wasn't much room in the back alley for the two of us, let alone the crowd that had gathered. Fluffy had a fat butt, which slowed him down. His love of cupcakes and the forty years he had on me didn't help him much. The thinner air up here in Denver wasn't exactly treating me well, either.

"I'm going to gnaw your bones into splinters." Fluffy's words came out in a raspy snarl.

If it weren't for Fuzz warning me ahead of time that Fluffy was a skinwalker, I'd have been shocked the first time he spoke.

"I always wondered if your kind eats humans." I pretended to shudder. "That's cannibalism, you know?"

He clawed the ground.

"Tell me who you work for, Fluffy, and I may let you walk away from this fight."

His growl vibrated in my chest. "I work for no man."

"Man? Nah, I'm looking for a demon with black soulless eyes, a fancy suit, and a thing for stealing young girls."

The golden glow of his eyes dimmed. "That describes quite a few of my friends."

"Yes, but you're the lapdog for only one of them," I said.

The upper lip of his middle head curled back to reveal a set of wicked canines. I had no intention of tangling with those again.

"Suit yourself." I pushed off the wall to saunter toward him.

He watched the sway of my hips in the tight leather pants I wore. The metal clasps of my biker boots jingled with each step. The shredded remains of my black tank hung from my chest. A new layer of skin had begun to form over his telltale claw marks.

Fluffy sniffed the air when I stopped less than five feet from him. His sneeze coated me with slime.

"Gross." I wiped my face clean.

"I knew it. I suspected earlier that you weren't human." All three heads dipped low to glare at me. "I'm allergic to only one creature: birds."

I met his condemning gaze. "Do I look like a bird to you?"

"You're a shifter."

I laughed. "If I were, don't you think I would've shifted by now?"

He rolled his eyes to look back at Fuzzbert. "You may not be a shifter, but you aren't human, either."

I'd always known I was different. Healing wasn't the only ability I possessed. I also had a way with fire.

"What's it to you?" I crossed my arms and jutted out one hip.

His laugh made the hair on the back of my neck rise. "Foolish girl. A skinwalker's bite leaves more than a scar."

"You son of a—" My arms fell to my sides. "You bit me, knowing I'd turn into your kind?"

It was sickening, barbaric even. It was also annoyingly brilliant. Not that I would tell him that.

"You chose me as your opponent, remember?" His heads fell in line with each other so his statement sounded in stereo. "The risk was yours to take."

"Bastard," I muttered under my breath. I took hold of his center head. His fur crawled with bugs where I buried my hands to reach the skin. "Give me a name."

Heat flooded into my palms. It started with a familiar tingle but rapidly built to a blistering heat. Steam rose from his wet pelt. The wolf's laugh cut off, and his screams began.

The teeth of his left head sank deep into my arm. Blood flowed around the wounds. His hindquarters slammed into the alley wall. Mortar gave way in chunks, coating his back.

"What's going on over there?"

Fuzzbert's heavy footsteps headed our way.

"Give me his name." I tightened my grip, and the scent of

burning fur filled my nose. Pain flared in my shoulder when Fluffy's third head attacked. His teeth ripped at muscle and scored bone. The pain made my vision darken, but I held on.

"Let him go," Fuzzbert demanded.

"Stay out of this, Fuzz. I don't want to hurt you."

"Hurt me?" The troll rocked to a stop. "Have you lost your ever-loving mind, girl? I could grind you into dust in seconds."

I released one hand holding Fluffy and pointed it at Fuzz. Fire erupted in the palm of my hand. A swirling ball of vibrant orange hovered there. In the very center of the flames was a blue so bright, it forced Fuzzbert to look away.

"What are you?" the troll asked from behind the shield of his hand.

That I didn't know. I'd spent years looking for the answer. So far, all I had were questions.

"Get her off me," Fluffy whimpered.

Where I'd gripped Fluffy, the imprint of my palm was beginning to heal. I needed to remain in constant contact with him.

Fuzzbert inched forward. With each step he took, the flames rose higher from my hand. "I don't want any trouble, Fuzz."

"You've got a fine way of showing that."

I broke eye contact with Fluffy to look at the troll. "This man knows who killed my momma. I'm not leaving until he gives me a name."

"Bugger." Fuzzbert rubbed the back of his head, forgetting that he wore a poncho.

"Don't just stand there. Do something!" Fluffy moaned.

Digging my nails into Fluffy's neck drew out a terrible howl. The heat cauterized on contact. His eyes rolled back. The scent of his burnt hair was thick in the air.

Murmurs rippled through the crowd. Several pressed against the protective barrier hiding us from the humans. The mages on Fuzzbert's payroll had to work harder to keep us hidden.

No amount of warding could shield Fluffy's frenzy. His thrashing sent tremors through the concrete. Screeching yelps of pain echoed out of the alley. The doorman standing in front of the small condo building across the street peered into the dark. He couldn't see us. Not yet, at least.

"This is getting out of hand," the troll said, surveying his paying crowd. He was losing them. "Tell her what she wants to know, then bite her head off."

The wolf's eyes glistened with tears. "He'll kill me for saying!"

Fuzzbert gave him a withering glare. "If you finish her off, no one will know but you and me. My silence comes at a very fair price."

That was loyalty for you. It started and ended with the highest bidder.

The stench of fear and urine rose from Fluffy. I wondered if the enchantment could hide that smell, too.

"You'll let me live?" He yipped as flames curled the ends of his fur, spreading out from my hands.

I'd heard my fair share of the tales of his exploits in the human world. He was filth, undeserving of life. But he still had his uses.

I nodded, not trusting myself to say the words in case I changed my mind later. Fluffy sniffed and raised one head, turning it in the direction of the crowd.

"They won't help you," I said and followed his gaze. The vampires in attendance might pay a good price for Fluffy's blood if I decided to fry him.

I wonder if he would taste like a human or an animal to them.

I knew very little about the Navajo legends of such creatures. Only that they were once human—witches who turned only after killing someone close to them. Or at least, that was one rumor floating around. This particular legend was very sensitive to the Native American tribes. So, during my travels, I steered far away from it, out of respect.

There were a couple of shifters in the group that might attack if I did kill him. Even though a skinwalker wasn't the same species, they might stick together. I'd seen pack mentality cross species lines before.

"Quiet!" Fuzzbert shouted to the nervous crowd. Whatever he was trying to hear, I was sure his elephant ears would pick it up. "I hear it, too."

It took another minute for me to hear the sirens.

"Who called the pigs?" A tiny faerie of some sort, sitting on the shoulder of a man at the front, fluttered her wings with agitation.

"Maybe they aren't coming our way." A small goblin beside the faerie wrung his hands. He wore a little suit coat. The glint of a golden pocket watch caught my eye. Fuzzbert was too panicked to notice this tempting treasure.

Another flare from my hand sent Fluffy into spasms hard enough to crack the brick wall. The metal scaffolding fixed to the front of the building collapsed to the street. A great puff of dust burst across the entrance to the alleyway. Pieces of the historic landmark crumbled. The doorman dove for the phone, ensuring that the police would be coming.

That was exactly the advantage I needed.

Purchase *From the Embers* by Amy Miles at your favorite book retailer.

www.ingramcontent.com/pod-product-compliance
Lightning Source LLC
Chambersburg PA
CBHW031319280626
47169CB00019B/2185